Jamila Gavin

When I am asked if the Surya Trilogy is autobiographical, the answer is yes and no. Yes, that I couldn't have written it had I not been born in India into the period leading up to the Second World War, independence and partition; yes, that as a child I lived both in a palace in the Punjab and in a drab flat in a war-damaged London street; yes, that music, sea voyages, schools, friends were all part of my rich Anglo-Indian existence. But no – in any accurate sense to do with the plot or events as described in the books. Everything I experienced simply became material with which I could overlay a complete fantasy. As a child can turn a table into a house or two chairs into a train, I turned my life into a fiction in which any resemblance to characters living or dead is purely coincidental – as they say in the movies.

Also in the Contents series

Contents

The Eye of the Horse

JAMILA GAVIN

mammoth

To Miriam – The hub of the wheel holds all its parts together

The Collected Poems and Plays of Rabindranath Tagore published by Macmillan

First published in Great Britain in 1994
by Methuen Children's Books Ltd
Mammoth paperback edition first published 1995
Reissued 1997 by Mammoth
an imprint of Reed International Books Ltd
Michelin House, 81 Fulham Road, London SW3 6RB
and Auckland and Melbourne

Copyright © 1994 Jamila Gavin

The moral rights of the author and cover illustrator have been asserted.

ISBN 0 7497 2396 3

10 9 8 7 6 5 4 3 2 1

A CIP catalogue record for this title is available
from the British Library

Printed and bound in Great Britain
by Cox & Wyman Ltd, Reading, Berkshire

Contents

Then they let loose a white horse. And it was
decreed that, wheresoever this horse should
wander, King Rama would follow, even to the ends
of the earth, until he might be led to the only
person who could forgive him.

Ramayana

ONE

The Omen

'Hey, Bublu! I heard something!'

The youngest boy, Sparrow, leaned over and shook the oldest boy.

'Shut up, will you,' groaned Bublu. It was hard enough to sleep at the best of times without being woken deliberately, what with the bitter winter cold and the fretful whimperings and nightmares, which racked them all on most nights.

Bublu enshrouded himself more tightly in the thin cotton sheet. He tried to ease the agony of the hard stone floor beneath his body, by rolling himself half over the limbs of the other boys. There was a murmuring of grunts and muttered protests, as everyone readjusted themselves in the knotted huddle they had formed around the ashes of last night's fire.

But Bublu was awake now, and a few moments later, he too heard a noise. His body tensed automatically.

'See! Didn't I tell you?' hissed Sparrow, his cold face pressed to Bublu's ear. 'You heard it, didn't you! Is it them again? Are they coming to kill us?' His voice almost broke out loud with panic.

Bublu clamped his hand over the youngest boy's

mouth. 'Shut up, won't you!' He whispered. 'All that's over now.' Even so, he was fully alert and sat up swiftly in the darkness, his mind already assessing the escape routes. He and the boys had gone over them many times, working out all the possible strategies. They had explored every part of the deserted palace; all the rooms, chambers, passageways, stairways; the different levels of terraces and even the wild saplings and creepers, down which they could shin in an emergency.

He listened, not breathing. In the past, the speed of his decision had been the difference between life and death.

They heard it again. It sounded like air being puffed out through nostrils; it was like the soft snort of a beast.

He hadn't realised that Sparrow had clasped him round the waist, terrified that, should there be an order to flee, he would be left behind. Bublu struggled to his feet with Sparrow still clinging to him and shifted the child to his hip. 'Hush, kid! Take it easy, it's just an animal. Let's go and look.'

'What if it's Muslims?' stammered Sparrow.

'Arreh!' breathed Bublu, his sound smiling in the darkness. He was a Muslim.

Although it was pitch black, Bublu's senses were so finely tuned that he knew in which direction was the doorway out onto the great verandah. Very rapidly, his eyes adjusted and he was able to differentiate between the inner darkness of the room in which they were sleeping, and the paler black of the starry night outside.

Sparrow was shaking uncontrollably with cold and fear as Bublu tiptoed to the entrance. A low half-moon came into view, casting a soft glow over the marble terrace. He stepped over the threshold and at first saw nothing but the great vast canopy of trees and undergrowth, which had grown out of control and turned the palace garden into a wilderness. Then there was a slight scrape of hoof on stone. The animal stood motionless, right there at the top of the verandah steps. At first he thought it was one of the palace statues, gleaming as white as the mist which hung over the lake beyond. But then the creature snorted again, and pawed the ground.

'It's a horse!' exclaimed Bublu incredulously. 'What the heck is a horse doing round here!' Before he could utter another word, the animal leapt off the verandah and galloped away into the night.

The horse was seen again just before dawn of the next day.

It was Tuesday, 13 January 1948.

It materialised out of the frosty darkness, its hooves echoing strangely on the long white road. It was a pale horse; white as jasmine; white as the fresh snows on the mountain peaks to the north; white as the road beneath its feet.

Although the bridle had been fitted to a bit in its mouth, it had no saddle, and the reins hung loose. It looked to all intents and purposes like a bridegroom's horse, for garlands of freshly threaded flowers hung round its neck, and a fringe of miniature pearls swung across its brow.

Sleepy farmers, startled out of their huddled blankets, saw it as they drove their bullock carts one behind the other, on their long trek to market. They called out to each other in the chilly darkness, standing up on the wooden yoke which held their beasts in harness.

'Did you see that?' they called.

'Was it a horse?'

'Whose is it? Where does it come from?'

One of them leapt from his cart and tried to grab it, but the horse reared in the air, shook him off, and galloped away.

The teacher glimpsed it as he cycled to school. It was mirrored in the dark, stagnant water of a ditch by the side of the road, its head stooped low to drink.

Old Ram Singh who, after his house had been razed to the ground, had made his home in the abandoned shell of All Souls' Church, saw it grazing among the scarred and desecrated tombstones in the graveyard.

All that day the horse was seen, here and there, trotting along the dykes, meandering among the fields and nuzzling at fruit, which hung from the lower boughs in the guava groves. Sometimes it drifted tantalisingly close to the old men smoking their hookahs outside their homes, or the women filling pitchers with water from the well.

Later, after sundown, in the yellow paraffin light of the tea houses in the town, the gossip was all about the horse. They argued about where it had come from, to whom it belonged and what they should do about it. Some confessed they had tried already to catch it, but without success.

Bublu, who came into town every day to hang about, kept his ears open. This must be the same horse he and Sparrow had seen in the night. If the horse were a runaway and if he caught it, he would have as much right to it as anyone else. He wandered up to Dilip Singh, the tea-shop owner. 'Here, let me hand out the tea while you fill the kettle again,' he offered ingratiatingly.

'Arreh! Everyone comes to me for a soft touch,' Dilip Singh grumbled, but let Bublu hand out the cups anyway. The old-timers, those who had survived the troubles, knew the boy as Nazakhat Khan, son of the Muslim tailor, but they pretended not to, for his own safety.

'The horse must have come down out of the mountains,' said a farmer, as Bublu put a cup of tea before him. They all glanced to the northern horizon, where even in the darkness, the distant peaks of the Himalayas gleamed, everlastingly white.

'Maybe it belongs to a Kashmiri trader,' suggested a voice.

'I say it's a bridal horse that's run off,' declared another. 'Didn't you see how decorated it was?'

'I haven't heard of any weddings taking place today, have you?' said the proprietor.

'No! They say this month will not be auspicious,' old Sharma, the sadhu, warned with a shake of his head. 'There won't be many marriages in the next few weeks.'

Old Sharma, the holy man, was another who spent his days hanging round the tea houses, waiting for the farmers to come with their tales and chatter. One of them was always sure to give him a free cup of tea, and a samosa too, if he was lucky. He shook his head like a grizzled prophet. 'It's an omen,' he warned. 'You mark my words. There has been too much killing. The gods must come now and take their retribution.'

'Hey, Sharma, don't bring talk like that into my tea house. You've had your cup, you old scrounger, now get out!' yelled Dilip Singh. He grabbed the sadhu by the scruff of the neck and pushed him out on to the road.

The farmers looked at each other and shrugged. 'Dilip Singh's conscience is getting him ruffled!' they smirked, though they all knew that no one's hands were clean.

'Hey, *Babuji*,' cried Bublu, running over to help the old sadhu to his feet. 'Do you mean it? Is the horse a bad omen?'

'Ugh! Good, bad! How should I know? An omen is an omen.'

The dusty wireless, connected by a long twisted flex into the light socket and draped in wilting marigolds like a neglected goddess, crackled out news from New Delhi.

'Shush!' yelled a voice. 'Listen! Listen, you chattering oafs!'

The voices quietened. They turned their ears to

the smooth, anglicised tones of All India Radio which emanated from the temple of sound, propped on the shelf between the bags of spices.

Bublu didn't understand English. 'What is he saying?' he pleaded.

'Just be quiet, boy,' muttered one of them. 'How can we tell with you chattering on.'

'This morning at eleven o'clock our respected Gandhiji began a fast. He told us of his profound sorrow that there is still so much communal strife in the country. It is his aim to achieve a reunion of hearts of all communities, with God as his supreme and sole counsellor.'

'Did you hear that?' the farmers whispered. 'Gandhiji is fasting again.' They gazed at each other, their faces etched with anxiety. The troubles were still all around them, they knew that. Every day there were reports of slayings and revenge. They glanced uneasily at old Sharma who was rubbing his elbows and brushing off the dust from his thin, spindly body.

'What's happening?' begged Bublu, seeing the startled concern on everyone's faces.

'It's the Mahatma, he's going to fast again.'

'What will be left of his body,' exclaimed a voice. The Mahatma was so small, so frail already. It was inconceivable that his skeletal frame could cope with any more deprivation.

'How can we see a future for India and Pakistan once the British have left, if everyone is at each other's throats?' Gandhi had asked. 'If this is the

9

only way to make the politicians see sense then so be it.'

And so, once more, the Mahatma offered himself as a sacrifice.

That evening, Bublu got the boys to make a bigger fire than usual. The sadhu's talk of omens and retribution had made him feel uneasy. Even though he was on home ground; even though he had been born in the village, as had previous generations of his family, ever since the troubles had broken out, Bublu had become a stranger – an alien in his own land. No one looked him in the eye, not even those who had known him all his life. His family had all been killed right here among them, and now, it was as if they had never been.

Somehow surviving, he slunk round the district with a raggle-taggle of other boys, who had also been orphaned or displaced. They stuck together in a band and set up camp in the ruined palace. No one else went there because of the ghosts and evil spirits that were reputed to haunt it.

The boys all had nicknames too, so that they could not be easily identified by race or creed. Bublu was the eldest and a natural leader, after having fought it out with Sandeep, whom they called One Eye – though he still had to watch his old rival.

They usually all straggled back to the ruined palace before sunset, bringing with them whatever gains they had collected through the day. It became the code of the group to pool everything – scraps of clothes, materials, objects – anything that might come in useful as a tool or a receptacle; and of course, each knew he must bring something back to contribute to a meal. The boys had agreed on a law: stealing vegetables and sugar cane from the fields was one thing – or scrumping mangoes, guavas and bananas, strictly for their own consumption – but there was to be no stealing from houses or persons. Any boy breaking the code would be punished by the group and if necessary, thrown out.

They were never sure each evening what, if anything, they would eat. Someone usually managed to break off some sugar cane, scrounge discarded radish tops or old chapattis, and if they were lucky, one or two women in the village left out some rice or lentils which the boys cooked up in an old petrol can.

Gradually, they became as tolerated in the district as the crows and stray dogs, which scavenged round the neighbourhood. But Bublu never dropped his guard – not with anyone.

Tonight, Bublu was ever more alert. Kept awake, not by strange noises or the fretful moanings of his companions, but the feeling that, somewhere out in the darkness, the white horse still roamed like an unquiet spirit.

However, his mind was made up. If he got the chance, he was going to catch it.

TWO

The Sacrifice

The clerk's wife sighed. Her three fat sons clustered round her with pouting faces. Her husband had insisted that they too must fast. 'It is our duty to support the Mahatma,' explained the clerk.

'Why, Pa?' protested the eldest fat son. 'How does it help the cause?'

'After all, he won't know,' said the second fat son. 'No one will know.'

'Except us and our empty stomachs,' moaned the third fat son.

But the clerk mercilessly reduced his family's diet to a handful of nuts and one piece of fruit per day, saying, 'At least you won't starve like Gandhiji. He's taking nothing, only water.'

It was too bad the way he carried his adoration of the Mahatma to such extreme limits and it wasn't fair on the boys. The clerk's wife gazed with anguished adoration at her three beautiful sons, as chubby as the god Ganesh and triumph of her womb.

They were a good Hindu family belonging to the Shatryia caste, who had managed to survive the troubles. They had only left the district temporarily when first Muslim, then Sikh gangs rampaged through. But as things quietened down, they returned to rebuild their home, and re-establish their place in the community.

Surely, they were entitled to some dignity? After all, they had to think of their reputation, and the future wives they would need to find for the boys. Yet since the clerk's conversion to Gandhism he had stripped their modest home of everything that he called luxuries; their bedsteads, chairs, tables, ornaments, rugs – all had been given away or disposed of. He forbade his wife to wear jewellery and made her give away her best silk saris. From now on, they slept on thin mattresses on rickety charpoys, and all of them wore garments made from khadi, the raw rough cotton which had been spun by hand in the villages. She was sure the tailor had smirked when instructed to make their outfits.

Their food too had to be the most humble; just dhal, yogurt, fruit and nuts. No spices, no flavourings and no sweets were allowed.

His children were outraged. Three shiny plump boys, with cheeks like golden butter, who had been nourished and pampered from birth, with lashings of rich milk, cream, butter and cheese; who were used to curries cooked in the highest quality ghee, and ate only the freshest vegetables and fruit, and the finest white rice: whose mother adored making sweets and pastries and savoury samosas – they were to be denied all this – anything that smacked of pleasure or frivolity was banned. Food was for survival, because that was the lot of the poor, and it was with the poor that the clerk forced the whole family to identify.

Whenever they travelled by train, he insisted they cram themselves into the overflowing third class, along with malodorous peasants with their bundles and baskets.

But quite the worst indignity of all, was that the clerk made his wife clean out the latrines – the job of an Untouchable. She had begged and pleaded and screamed, and even threatened to leave home, but to no avail. The clerk told her that Gandhi had declared caste to be evil and must be done away with; that there was no longer any such thing as an 'Untouchable'. People, who until now had been the lowest of the low – so low that they were outside caste itself, fit only to do the most menial of jobs, they were now to be called 'Harijans' – 'children of God'. Everyone is equal in the eyes of God, Gandhi said, and he made his own wife clean out the latrines.

'If Gandhi's wife can clean out the latrines, then so can you,' intoned the clerk without sympathy. 'It is God's work the same as everything else.'

'Then why don't you do it,' hissed his wife under her breath.

'What did you say?' asked the clerk looking up from *The Times of India* he was reading.

'I didn't speak,' murmured his wife, hurrying away with furious tears streaming down her face. What did he care that none of her women friends would come to take tea with her any more? And she was sure that her own children flinched from her when she kissed them.

Luckily for the three fat boys, the fast only lasted five days, but they made up for it by secretly buying sweets and *gelabees* from the sweet-seller, whom they passed each day on their way to school. Their mother always made sure they had enough annas in their pockets for whatever extra food they wanted to buy in the bazaar.

During that time, the horse was still to be seen in the district, though only fleetingly.

Gandhi ended his fast on Sunday, 18 January 1948.

THREE

The Gardens of Treachery

At early evening, just before the chill of night, the schoolteacher had taken to walking in the neglected, overgrown gardens of the abandoned palace. He sometimes took a small volume of poetry to read, relishing the loneliness which enabled him to declame it out loud.

'There is a looker-on who sits behind my eyes.
It seems he has seen things in ages and worlds beyond memory's shore,
And those forgotten sights glisten on the grass and shiver on the leaves.'

At the end of an avenue, just where it ran down to the lake shore, was a stone plaque, now quite hidden by tangled creepers. He found it by accident, when a loose page from his book blew into the undergrowth, and he was forced to leave the grassy track to retrieve it. Earth had already crept halfway up the hard, grey granite, almost obliterating the letters carved deeply into its surface. But he had scraped away the soil to reveal words. They were in English. First were two names: 'Ralph and Grace'. These were the English children, the Chadwicks' children, who had drowned in the lake some years ago. Many would go nowhere near the place now, for there had been talk of their ghosts walking on the water and the sound of childish laughter on the island in the middle of the lake. Beneath the names, chiselled deep and in a fine hand, were the words of a poem, also in English but dedicated to Lord Shiva:

> I searched for your light
> Everywhere:
> And saw a dawn made from ten million
>   million suns,
> A cosmic brightness for my wonder.
>
> O Destroyer of Darkness
> If you are light
> I need look no more.

That evening he walked in the cool, fragrant gardens. Just as he passed the plaque, and repeated the now well-remembered words, the schoolteacher had a sudden feeling that he was not alone.

Turning slowly, with a sharp chill running up his spine, he saw by the lake shore, some hundred metres away, the white horse. It was still bridled, and the garlands of flowers which hung round its neck looked as fresh as ever.

But there was something else now. Crouched nearby, as though it were its keeper, squatted a child all naked and wild, with hair that fell around it in a matted, tangled mass. Whether it was a girl or a boy, he could not tell, or perhaps, after all, it wasn't human. Perhaps it was some animal, a monkey or even a young hyena, for when it suddenly looked up at him, it seemed to catch his eye with a glittering stare, and even from that distance, the look was so savage that he shuddered.

After a while, the horse moved on around the shore. The creature followed, sometimes on all fours, sometimes bounding about on two. The teacher watched them till they disappeared round a promontory. They did not reappear, although he waited until the sun had almost set.

It was Thursday, 29 January 1948.

'*Well, my daughter Marvi, and what are you doing today?*'

Jhoti asked the same question almost every morning, just at the point of waking, before Marvinder had even opened her eyes.

'I like Wednesdays, Ma,' whispered Marvi into the cold, winter darkness. She could just see her breath puff upwards like a coil of ectoplasm, towards the still invisible ceiling. 'We have our singing lessons with Mr Pentelow. He's nice. He lets us choose our favourites.'

'*What is your favourite, Marvi, my dearest?*' sighed her mother. '*Is it the song of spring which the farmers sing on their way to the fields? Is it the song about Krishna, stealing milk from the milkmaids? They were my favourites too.*'

'No, Ma. We don't sing those songs here in England. We sing "The Ash Grove" and "Men of Harlech" and songs about Scotland. My favourite

18

song is "Speed Bonnie Boat like a Bird on the Wing." '

Marvinder began to sing it quietly, sliding down under the bedclothes, so that she wouldn't waken Kathleen and Beryl.

'You're going to be a musician, aren't you, Marvi?' Her mother sounded proud. 'A violinist like Mr Chadwick, aren't you, my daughter, aren't you, my precious?'

'Dr Silbermann teaches me well, Ma. I wish you could hear me.'

'Do you remember, how we sat on the verandah in Deri, and listened, while Jaspal suckled at my breast? Do you remember, Marvinder, my child? Every evening, before dinner, the Chadwicks made music?'

'Yes, Ma,' cried Marvinder, and the tears slid down her cheeks. How could she forget? The music rose through the scented air of a Punjab evening, lifting out of the boughs of the mission garden like spirit birds, soaring and dipping and disappearing on and on into space. Even though they now lived in England, how could she forget? Especially not now that her mother, Jhoti, had taken up residence in her brain.

Marvinder had been dreaming about a horse. Sitting astride a white horse, she had been galloping . . . galloping . . . along twisting mountain trails; jumping gulleys and ditches and bubbling streams; ducking her head beneath the low branches of pine and spruce; then breaking out onto an open plain, where a silver horizon ran unimpeded from end to end; where the wind caught the horse's tail and made it fan out behind it like a silver cataract; and her heart beat with the drumming of its hooves, as they sped along so fast, that any minute now, she felt they would leap up into the skies and gallop away among the stars.

But the sounds which awoke her were slow and heavy. Marvinder heard the early morning clip clop of the milkman's cart coming down to Whitworth Road, and the faint tinkle of bottles as he unloaded the quota destined for No. 30.

She eased herself silently out of bed and sped, barefoot, down the freezing lino-covered stairs, to the front door. She opened it in time to see the milkman climbing the front steps with cheery face beaming out at her from beneath his peaked cap.

'Hello, my little early bird,' he whispered, as with practised silence, he set down the various groups of milk bottles in their proper places. 'Looking for worms?'

She grinned back, remembered how it was he who taught her the saying, 'it's the early bird that catches the worm'.

Then, suddenly, his face became grave, and he bent forward confidentially. 'There was news on the wireless this morning that'll interest you,' he murmured.

'Oh?' Marvinder was puzzled.

'Mahatma Gandhi.' The milkman said the name with reverence. 'He's been shot.'

It was Friday, 30th January 1948.

So, Marvinder in England heard the news before the clerk in India. The clerk didn't hear till almost evening. He had been accounting all day, sitting in front of large dusty ledger books, with his specs balanced on his nose, pencil in hand, roaming up and down columns of figures, calculating, adding and subtracting and dividing, his brain revolving and clicking like the beads on an abacus.

'What do you want?' he demanded of the gangly youth who lingered somewhat insolently in the doorway.

The clerk knew he was something of a laughing-stock with his colleagues, who liked to tease him for being such a faithful disciple of the Mahatma – especially as he came to work wearing a coarse khadi dhoti, instead of refined white cotton trousers and shirts or even western-style suits. What's more, he had insisted on removing the top of his desk from its frame, placing it on the floor and working cross-legged. 'We Indians should do things the Indian way, not ape the Britishers,' he had declared with an air of moral superiority. However, it irked him no end, to think that he was being smirked at behind his back, by the cocky young messengers who hung about the office.

'You haven't heard the news, then?' asked the youth with mock concern.

'What news?' The clerk frowned. He straightened his back from his cross-legged position, and adjusted his spectacles which had slipped down his nose. As he did so, he was aware of the sound of women wailing in the background and agitated voices, rising and falling in repeating sequences of distress. Anxiously, he gathered up his dhoti and got to his feet.

'It's your beloved leader; the Father of the People ... Bapu ...' The youth drawled out the words slowly and sarcastically, relishing the puzzled anxiety he could see beginning to furrow the clerk's face.

'Gandhiji? Gandhiji?'

'He's been shot!'

'Is he dead?'

'Oh yes.' The youth tittered, then fled.

Slipping ... slipping ... the ground was slipping away from beneath his feet. The clerk clutched his heart and then his head. The whole world became dark and began to spin around him as if out of control ... it was a past betrayed ... a future lost ... what would happen ... what would become of them? All that slaughter ... destruction ... and a terrible sickness of the soul ... who could heal the wounds? Who could save them now? What revenge would God take for the death of a saint? Slipping ... slipping ... there was nothing solid for his feet to stand on.

The clerk crumpled to the ground, his arms clutched around his head as if waiting to be sucked away into oblivion.

In his distraught mind, he wandered through beautiful gardens of ornamental lakes and perfumed fountains; down shaded avenues of cypresses; into fruit groves and walled gardens, where flowering bushes were bursting with colour

22

and profusion. They were gardens of order and peace created out of a jungle of danger and chaos. Yet a voice whispered in his brain. Beware! Beware the beast that lurks; the enemy disguised as a friend; the serpent coiled among the boughs of the tree in the garden of Eden, waiting for Eve; beware the Judas seeking out Jesus in the Garden of Gethsemane to embrace him with the kiss of betrayal; Ravana, king of the demons disguised as a holy man; the devil who has gained access into the inner sanctuary.

But it was too late for warnings. In a garden in Delhi, an assassin lurked among the shrubberies of Birla House. A man, pretending to be a disciple, waited for Gandhi.

The Mahatma was still frail and impossibly thin after his long fast. Flanked by his faithful women followers, on whose shoulders he rested a hand for support, he walked trustingly to a prayer meeting. The assassin stepped forward. So close. As close as friends. He faced him, looked him in the eye, then shot him three times.

'Hiya Ram, Ram, Ram!' were the last words on the Mahatma's dying breath.

'The light has gone out of our world,' wept the Prime Minister.

Later that day the horse was seen again, galloping in a frenzy down the long white road. Some said a strange rider crouched on its back; some demented creature with wild hair flying – small as a child or a hunchback.

23

But that night, the horse came again to the palace. Bublu heard its footfall on the terrace. Bublu moved with the silence of a hunter. This time, he would catch it. He heard its breath and saw its white shape gleaming in the darkness. It looked up. The horse saw him with glittering eye. It didn't run away. Bublu held out a hand of friendship. 'Come to me, my beauty! Don't run away. Come to me, O wondrous one!'

As he spoke, he moved closer and closer. Now he could feel its warm breath as he held his hand up to its nostrils. He stroked its nose and murmured lovingly to it. 'Let's be friends. Stay with me. I'll feed you and groom you and ride you well. Stay, my beauty.'

The horse stood stock-still. Then Bublu realised that, sheltering beneath the horse's belly, protected between its four legs, crouched a creature with long wild hair. In the darkness, he couldn't make out the face, but its eyes, like the eyes of a snake, stared at him, glittering and hypnotic.

Bublu cried out loud with shock, but still the horse didn't move.

What had come to them? What was this creature? Was it a demon? Was the horse a bringer of bad luck? Bublu remembered the words of the old sadhu.

He dared not move either towards the horse or back to his place by the fire. Instead, wrapping his sheet around him, Bublu sank down on his haunches, and stayed like that for the rest of the night, with his head sunk on to his arms.

FOUR

Train Tracks

Jaspal leaned over the old metal bridge and looked down onto the railway tracks below. The shining metal slithered away like parallel serpents, till they reached a point in the distance where they merged as if one – but he knew that this was only an optical illusion.

The sight of the tracks always gave him an intense feeling of excitement. Sometimes, when the sun was shining in a particular way, he could block from his view the grubby backs of those London houses and flats, with their grimy windows and straggles of grey washing hung out to dry. He could fix his eye on the patch of blue sky between the tenements, and imagine he was back in India. For a while, he could try and forget the pain which sat in his stomach like a hard lump.

Trains reminded him of his village back home in Deri. Beyond the mango and guava groves and between the fields of wheat, mustard seed and sugar cane, the railway track ran the length of the Punjab skyline.

He and his best friend, Nazakhat, had loved trains. On many an afternoon after school, they would take the long way home so that they might

25

get over to the track and walk on the rails. There was no chance of being run down by a train, as you could see as far as the horizon in each direction. Anyway, long before the train was in sight, you could feel the hum of its power beneath your feet. It was often the smoke they saw first, streaming a long trail in the sky, and then they would hear the piercing shriek of its whistle, which carried all the way to the village.

Although there was no need for danger, they often created it.

'Let's see who'll jump off first,' Jaspal had shrieked to his friend, as the train came nearer. They had waited and waited, giggling and wobbling about with arms outstretched for balance, each on his rail. Jaspal was to leap off on one side, Naza-khat to the other. As the train bore down on them, the engine driver would often be leaning out of his cab swearing and cursing at them, shaking his fist and telling them to get out of the way. But they would just shake their fists back, mouthing unmentionable insults and then, at the last minute, fling themselves aside.

Jaspal smiled at the memory. If only it was only the good times he remembered. But trains pounded through his dreams at night. Indian trains, filled with refugees, escaping from the mayhem which was caused when India was split into two to create Pakistan; when Muslims, Hindus and Sikhs set upon each other with vicious fury, and people were driven hither and thither. The shriek of the train whistle had been a scream of death; a scream of hatred and murder and massacre. He had seen it. The images would never go away, though he tried to forget. He tried to forget the day they fled from their village. He, his sister, his grandmother and mother set off for Bombay. His mother, Jhoti, had been saving small amounts of money each time Govind sent anything from England. She had this dream, this conviction, that they would be able to buy themselves tickets on a ship bound for England. 'If your father won't come to us, then we will go to him,' Jhoti had declared. Such were the desperate times, everyone was rushing around trying to work out strategies for survival. There was no one to tell her whether or not she had enough money, what papers she would need or how she would get there. With thousands of others, she had simply set off for the nearest railway station.

In the pandemonium of overcrowded platforms and trains packed with refugees, Jhoti and her children were separated from each other. The force of the crush swept Jaspal and Marvinder onto a train, which then moved off, carrying them helplessly away. Now he and his sister Marvinder were here in England while their mother and grandmother had been left behind to an unknown fate. The pain of those memories was too much to bear. Mostly, he kept them locked away in the dark recesses of his mind. Better, instead, to remember his games and his friends – especially, Nazakhat.

There was a clicking sound of a signal being raised. A train must be coming. It would be the express bound for Bournemouth and the south coast. Jaspal felt the same old excitement. If only Nazakhat could see this. He pulled a notebook and pencil out of his pocket and heaved himself up onto the parapet, so that he could get a good view of the name and number of the engine. He could hear it now as it pounded nearer. A thrill of anticipation ran through him.

Suddenly a voice yelled over the increasing roar. 'Oi!' Jaspal dropped down and turned. 'Hey! Black-face! Bandage-head!' Johnnie Cudlip stood on the other side of the road, leering at him. Although he was only a little older than Jaspal, he was a big boy for his age. Taller by a head and shoulders than any of his peers, his body was clumsy and unwieldy, as if he wasn't sure what to do with it. His hands looked extra large, sticking out from the sleeves of the blazer he had outgrown six months ago.

Johnnie hated school because it made him feel stupid. Because teachers, who were hardly taller than he, crushed him with sarcasm and seemed to forget that, though he was as tall as a man, he was only a child. Out in the playground and the streets, it was a different story. There, he was king. There, he ruled. He was the leader of a terror gang. All the children feared him for his strength and the way he enjoyed a really good fight. What the teachers did with their tongues, he could do with his fists and feet and brute force. Anyone who wasn't with him was against him – and your life was hardly worth living if you weren't on his side – that is, until Jaspal came into the neighbourhood and soon formed a gang of his own.

Ever since Jaspal had moved into Whitworth Road, Johnnie had been out to get him; but though Jaspal was shorter than he, and thinner, somehow, Johnnie could never get to grips with him. He would no sooner jump on his back and get his head into a stranglehold, than Jaspal would wriggle like a fish, slither like a snake – somehow just make himself smaller and slip out of his grip. Other times, when the two boys would come face to face with each other, Jaspal's body seemed to solidify. He would stand upright, calm and still, except that the muscles in his neck were as taut as rope and his limbs all ready to strike like a whiplash. Many a time, Johnnie had set the gang on him, but Jaspal was fast, elusive and cunning. No one could outrun him. It was as if he could make himself invisible.

'Hanuman, Hanuman,' whispered their mother when Marvinder told her from inside her head. 'Hanuman, the son of Vayu, the god of the wind. He has magic powers – and not even the king of the demons can kill him. Hanuman found Sita. One day, he will find me.'

'You're like Hanuman,' Marvinder whispered to her brother, when she watched a gang fight one day on the common. It had been a brutal, bloody fight, but Jaspal couldn't be beaten. If he got knocked down, he was up on his feet again in a trice. He seemed to have eyes at the back of his head, and when his enemies came up behind him, he would start whirling his arms about and yelling like a mad creature.

Jaspal took up the name. He liked the sound it made. Hanuman . . . Hanuman . . . general of the king of the monkeys' army, fighter of demons; son of the wind god with powers to make himself invisible, or turn himself into any shape both big and small. He taught the word to his gang. Now, when they went into a fight, they would chant, Hanuman . . . Hanuman . . . Hanuman . . . and before they had even struck a blow, the sound of the chanting brought fear into the hearts of Johnnie Cudlip and his gang.

'Watching for the chuff-chuff, are we?' Johnnie sneered. Jaspal was alone. Alone, he looked small, thin and easy to bully. Taking advantage of a break in the traffic, Johnnie dashed over the road and stood menacingly close to Jaspal.

The train was hurtling closer in a great cloud of black steam and smoke. Jaspal would have to lean well over to see the number. It meant turning his back on Johnnie. He hesitated then, gripping the rail of the bridge, he heaved himself up to his armpits and, with his toes, found some rivets with which to steady himself. He leaned over as far as he dared. The engine smoke whirled about him. Suddenly he felt hands grip his legs. Johnnie tipped him so that he was almost see-sawing over the side.

'Need some help, do you?' taunted Johnnie, laughing fiercely.

Jaspal felt himself losing control as the train sped

beneath him, under the bridge. Instinctively, he clutched the sides with his hands and, in doing so, let slip his precious notebook, which contained pages and pages of numbers and the names of engines, taken down over hours of train-spotting. With a cry of anguish, he watched it fluttering down onto the track, just as the last carriage was sucked from view.

With miserable fury, Jaspal kicked out with all his might and sent Johnnie stumbling backwards, almost into the road. A bus blared out a warning on its horn, and someone shouted, 'Bloomin' rascals! Why aren't they in school?'

Free of Johnnie's grip, Jaspal ran to the far end of the bridge. All he could think about was retrieving his notebook. He discovered a small space between the edge of the bridge and a wall. He slid through and found himself on top of the steep embankment. There below him on the track he saw it, the wind idly riffling through its pages.

He began to slide down, partly on his bottom, struggling to keep control.

'You coolie. I'll get you for that!' Smarting from the indignity of being kicked into the gutter, Johnnie came slithering down the embankment after him.

Jaspal reached the track. Just then, they heard another whistle. A second train was coming. If he didn't get his notebook, it would be completely mangled beneath the wheels.

A goods train trundled into sight. It wasn't as fast as the express, but it was going at a fairly swift speed. Jaspal didn't hesitate. He dashed onto the line and grabbed the notebook. Johnnie too had now reached the edge of the track. Jaspal laughed and stood there, balancing on the rails brandishing his notebook. 'Did you want something, beanpole?' bellowed Jaspal. 'Well, come and get it!'

The train driver was blasting a warning on his whistle. He was only fifteen metres away. Jaspal didn't move. Johnnie made as if to run across. The driver blew his whistle again. Johnnie hesitated.

'Cowardy custard, can't eat mustard!' yelled Jaspal triumphantly. Johnnie flinched with horror as Jaspal threw himself off the track, a couple of metres from impact with the train.

The two boys stared at each other between the passing trucks. Their gaze burned with enmity; then, before the long trail of goods had gone by, Jaspal had vanished.

That evening, Jaspal and his gang gathered in the cellar of the bombed house at the end of the road. They were initiating a new member into their brotherhood. Jaspal, as leader, stood on a table to give him height and authority. He wore a black turban and Indian shirt and pyjamas. His ceremonial sword was visible where it was tucked into his belt. He stood with his arms folded and feet apart, like a Sikh warrior waiting for action. Two candles flickered, casting gigantic shadows against the stone walls and the boys below him were quiet and attentive, their shadowed features turned upwards expectantly. They didn't have turbans quite like Jaspal's, but they wore bandanas round their heads whenever they gathered together.

He looked down on his followers – about eight of them – their faces solemn and dedicated. Two of the gang stepped forward, flanking a thin, pale-faced boy who was blindfolded. One of the gang removed the blindfold, while another gave him his spectacles. The boy hastily crammed the spectacles onto his face, which gave him a startled expression and made him look scared. He was new to the area and had been tormented at school. He knew that the only way to survive was to get into one of the gangs, then at least he would have the protection of his own gang brothers. He glanced around him nervously, then looked down.

'What's your name?' demanded Jaspal.

'Gordon Collins.'

'To join this gang, you have to go through a test to prove you are brave and loyal. Do you understand?' Jaspal stared at him coldly.

'Yes.' Gordon tried to control his quavering voice and he kept his eyes firmly to the ground. What would they ask him to do? He had heard stories of terrible tasks to get into gangs – things that were dangerous or terrifying. He waited with dread.

'We have decided that you must spend the night in St Peter's Church alone, and whatever happens – whatever you see or hear – don't try and sneak out, because we'll know, and not only will you be banned from our gang, but we'll punish you for failing.'

Gordon heaved a sigh of relief, and looked round –

33

his glance seeming to say, 'Is that all?' He thought they might ask him to run across the railway track in front of an oncoming train, or to walk across the wall of the canal bridge in the dark. But there was a general intake of breath and a low murmuring from the gang members, as if they thought this was bad enough.

'When must I do it?' he asked.

'Tomorrow night,' answered Jaspal. 'Be outside the Palladium Cinema at ten o'clock sharp, and we will see you into the church. We'll be waiting for you when you come out in the morning – so don't think you can get away with anything. Understood?'

Gordon nodded. As he was escorted out of the cellar, he heard them chanting softly . . . Hanuman . . . Hanuman . . . Hanuman . . . They told him to scram. Until he was a gang member, he was not allowed to stay on for the meeting.

'Cor! Wouldn't like to be in your shoes,' hissed his escort, at the top of the steps. 'That church is haunted. I've heard of people who go grey with fright after spending a night in there.'

'I don't believe in ghosts,' declared Gordon stoutly, hoping that his shaking voice didn't give him away.

'Huh! Tell us that the day after tomorrow!' jeered the boys, pushing Gordon on his way.

'Right,' said Jaspal, jumping down from the table and sitting on it. 'Business. The Johnnie Cudlip gang attacked Ronnie, Teddy and Frank in Warley Grove last night.'

Everyone turned and sympathetically examined the cuts and bruises of three younger boys who sniffed and wiped their noses across their sleeves and grinned sheepishly.

'They're cowards, that lot, picking on the little ones. Got no guts to face us. I think we need to show 'em. We must draw the whole Cudlip gang out; plan an attack – an ambush – and fight them into surrender. It's about time Johnnie realised he can't keep messing us about. I say we fight them after school . . . down at the tracks. Put out the word.'

FIVE

The Prisoner

It was Saturday. Maeve Singh came downstairs and stood in the doorway of her parents' flat. Her body was still girlishly thin and undeveloped, as if she had grown up reluctantly. She held herself awkwardly stiff, like a tightly-coiled spring; her lips pressed together, her pretty face taut and defensive.

Her paper-white skin looked almost translucent as the sunlight fell across her face.

She was dressed to go out, though without much effort. She would have looked drab, except that the sun seemed to ignite the coils of red hair, which fell to her shoulders from beneath a panama-shaped green hat, and enriched the otherwise dull brown of her shapeless coat.

Her little daughter, Beryl, stood half-behind her, knee-high, clutching her mother's coat in one hand, while sucking her thumb through a tight fist, with the other. She wasn't dressed to go out, and knew that she was about to be left. Her light brown eyes shifted uneasily round the room, settling first on Jaspal, her half-brother. She was frightened of him. He always scowled and looked angry. He didn't like her, she knew that. He hardly ever looked at her.

Marvinder was different. Beryl loved her. Marvinder seemed pleased to have a sister, even if she was only a half-sister. But Beryl would get used to being only half; half a sister, half-Indian, half-Irish ... not as wholly Indian as their father, Govind, and not as wholly Irish as her mother, Maeve. Her skin was neither white nor brown; her hair neither black nor red. Only her eyes, her pale, flecked-brown eyes like the skins of almonds, were exactly the same as her father's eyes and exactly the same as Marvinder's. But she would not know this yet. She didn't look in mirrors – at least not to assess herself. Her mirror was other people, and she saw herself the way they saw her.

'Are you ready?' Maeve asked. There was no enthusiasm in her voice.

Jaspal, Marvinder and Maeve's young sister, Kathleen, had been lolling in front of the fire, engrossed in comics. Marvinder got up immediately, and pulled down her coat from the door, and Kathleen went over to her little niece, to coax her into staying. Jaspal rudely ignored Maeve and went on reading.

'Well, come on then,' Maeve was impatient. 'Get your coat on, Jaspal. We'll miss the bus. Good grief, we only go once a fortnight and, after all, it is to see your own father.' She almost spat out the word 'father' like a bitter pill.

'Can I go see Dadda!' wailed Beryl.

'Yeah, take Beryl. I don't want to go,' Jaspal muttered.

37

'Come on, *bhai*,' urged Marvinder, and she chucked his coat at him.

He reacted angrily. 'Look what you've done, you stupid idiot!' he yelled, dragging his comic out from under the coat. 'That's my comic. You've gone and wrecked my comic!'

Marvinder looked pained. Jaspal never used to talk rudely to her. 'It doesn't looked wrecked to me,' she retorted. 'Here!' She reached out to straighten it, but he whipped it away.

'Leave off. It's mine.'

'I know it's yours, silly! I was just going to smooth it out.'

Maeve ran over impatiently and snatched at the comic. 'For God's sake, Jaspal, will you stop messing around and come. We're going to miss the bus, I tell you.'

There was a ripping sound.

Jaspal gave a bellow of fury. 'Look what you've done! You've torn it . . . you . . .' He looked as if he would fly at her, but Marvinder grabbed his arm.

'Jaspal, no!' She begged, 'Just put on your coat and come.' She picked up his grey worsted coat and firmly held it out for him.

Jaspal snorted angrily and broke into a stream of Punjabi, which he knew infuriated Maeve. 'Why should I do what that woman wants? She's not my mother. She's nothing but a thief and a harlot, stealing away our father. Now she thinks she can lord it over us. Well, she can't. I don't have to do anything she says.'

'Oi, oi! You being rude again, you little devil?' It

38

was Mrs O'Grady appearing at the door. Her plump face was red with effort. She was panting heavily with having hauled two vast bundles of other people's laundry up the long flight of stairs. 'You needn't think I don't know what you're saying, just because you speak in your gibberish.' She dropped the washing and strode over to Jaspal with her hand raised. 'You get your coat on immediately or you'll get a clip round the ear.' She hovered over him, threateningly. 'And if I hear you've given Maeve any of your lip while out, Mr O'Grady will get his belt to you.'

That was no mean threat. One leg or no, Mr O'Grady was a powerful distributor of punishments, and even his strapping sons, Michael and Patrick, had to watch themselves when their father got mad.

Jaspal sullenly thrust his arms into the sleeves of the coat which Marvinder still held out for him, though when she tried to do up his buttons he pushed her away.

'I'll do it,' he growled. 'I'm not a baby.'

'Huh, I'm not so sure about that,' snapped Mrs O'Grady, lowering her hand. 'Now get off with you,' and she herded them to the landing, checking their hats and scarves and gloves and warning them about the chill out there.

If those who make up a family are like the spokes of a wheel, then Mrs O'Grady was both the hub and the outer rim. She held them all together; she fed them, nurtured them, washed and cooked for them and bullied them. She put up with her husband, with his drinking and temper and his fury at losing a leg in the war; she hustled her two boys, Patrick and Michael, making sure they got off to work every day – then taking half their wages at the end of the week, to store in the teapot which stood on the mantelpiece; and when Maeve had got pregnant by Govind – even though the man was a heathen and as brown as the River Thames, she insisted that the couple move into the household, taking the top-floor flat, which meant that the younger sister, Kathy, had to move down and sleep in the hall under the stairs.

In due course, when Beryl was born, it was Mrs O'Grady who coped, for Maeve was a reluctant mother, distraught at finding her freedom curtailed; and only a woman as mighty an Amazon as Mrs O'Grady could have endured the shock of finding out that Govind already had a wife and family back in India; only a woman with shoulders as broad as a continent could then take on his two refugee children, Jaspal and Marvinder, when they turned up out of the blue to find their father – a father who had got mixed up in black-marketeering and who was then sent to prison. She may have raged and grumbled and lashed out with her tongue, but she never complained. But kneeling in the darkness of the confessional, she had whispered to Father Macnally that she had prayed to the sweet Virgin not to send her any more children to look after – and especially, please – no more heathens.

'Mum!' Beryl wailed pathetically. She broke away

from Kathleen's arms and reached out for Maeve. 'I want to see Dadda. Take me too!'

Mrs O'Grady snatched up her grandchild and held her firmly, 'You stay with your Gran and your Aunty Kathleen, there's a duck. You can go next time.'

'We'll see you later, Beryl,' Maeve cooed at her child, trying to soften her voice and her face, before following Jaspal and Marvinder downstairs and out of the front door.

A sharp spring wind blew up Wandsworth High Road. It blew the scattered bus tickets into red, blue and yellow spirals and whirled them along the pavements. It made you hold on to your hat and clutch at your coat. It was the sort of wind which found its way into every crevice between neck and scarf, or wrist and glove. Even through the button-holes. They bent their heads before it as they walked to the bus stop; and turned their backs on it, as they waited and waited for the red double-decker to come.

They were grateful to the wind. At least it gave them an excuse not to talk. Instead, they buried their reddened chins into their scarves and collars and gazed wistfully down the road, as if their very concentration could will the bus to come quicker.

And when it came, roaring to a stop in response to their outstretched hands, they always went clattering up the metal spiral steps onto the top deck. Maeve liked to smoke.

Jaspal and Marvinder would rush for the seats up at the very front above the driver's head. They enjoyed the clear open view, and the feeling of being on top of the world. They could lean right forward and press their brows up against the glass.

But for all that, it was a gloomy journey which none of them relished. If only they could have got off at the river and spent the day in Battersea Park, or if, instead of changing buses at Hammersmith, they could have walked down to Shepherd's Bush market and milled around the hustle and bustle of the stalls. Instead, they had to watch it all slide by and listen to the monotonous warnings of the conductor. 'Hold very tight, please,' as he tugged on the lower-deck bell string. 'Ting, ting!' It was one ting to stop and two tings to go.

At last they reached Ducane Road. The vast open playing fields of Latymer School seemed to gather up the winds and hurl them into their faces.

That final walk always seemed the longest. Maeve walked a little ahead, as if embarrassed by them, looking fixedly in front, never addressing any remarks to them, as if afraid people might think they were her children.

Two groups of people walked the same pavement, but managed to create a meaningful distance between each other.

There were those whose destination was Hammersmith Hospital, and with whom Maeve tried to merge for most of the walk. They were a generally cheerful lot, clutching bunches of newly-bought flowers from strategically-placed flower-sellers, or brown paper bags full of whatever fruit they could obtain with their ration coupons.

This group pretended not to see the other group, with whom, for a while, they shared the same pavement and the same direction. Their eyes looked through them as though they were ghosts, and there was a certain smugness, when this first group branched off and poured through the gates of the hospital in time for visiting hours.

The second group pretended not to notice or care. Their faces were grimmer, their pace more reluctant. Hardly anyone spoke, but concentrated on coaxing their children along, or simply fixing their focus on the next main gateway, to which they finally came. And when they walked through, they kept their eyes lowered to the ground. They never looked up at the grim fortress towers of His Majesty's Prison, Wormwood Scrubs.

Here, Maeve, Jaspal and Marvinder joined a sizeable straggle of mostly women and children, gathering outside the large oval gate, waiting for the exact moment when they would be admitted. No matter how awful the weather, the gate was never opened even thirty seconds earlier than ordained.

Unlike hospital visitors, they weren't allowed to take in flowers or fruit or packages of food. Each was frisked at the gate; handbags were opened and searched. They were made to feel that by visiting a prisoner, the visitor too was somehow guilty.

After further hanging about, they were all finally ushered into a large room, supervised by blank-faced warders, where, waiting for them at a series of tables, were the prisoners, their eyes eagerly scanning the faces as they came in.

Marvinder saw her father.

He was thinner these days. Perhaps it was the way they cropped his hair very close to the head; it seemed to emphasise his gaunt face; it made his cheeks look more hollow. His skin was blanched as if deprived of sunlight.

Lately, he had become withdrawn. Marvinder wondered whether it was to do with the killing of Mahatma Gandhi. When they broke the news to him a couple of months back, he looked as if he were going to faint.

'Was he a very important man, Pa?' she had asked, when he had collapsed into his chair and thrust his head down on the table between his arms.

'Who can forgive me?' was all her father had been able to choke, as if he had been the assassin.

'*When he was a student your father admired Mahatma Gandhi; worshipped him like a saint,*' Jhoti had explained inside her daughter's head. '*He travelled miles to attend his gatherings, and then came back to the village with such stories. He would tell us that the British were going to leave, and that India would become independent; how this little, half-starved man, with only a piece of cloth round his middle, was standing up to the might of the British Empire. The whole village would gather round to listen. Your father was such an important person in those days. But now ... who would have thought ...*'

Marvinder waved a timid greeting. Her father raised a hand in acknowledgement. He stood up, but looked past her. He looked past Maeve too. It was Jaspal on whom he feasted his eyes. His gaze seemed to plead for understanding and forgiveness. 'Can't we be friends?'

But Jaspal lowered his eyes with embarrassment. It had been easy to love his father when he thought he was a hero. When they had lived in India, in their little Punjabi village, Jaspal, who had never known his father, grew up looking at the proud, flower-draped photograph, which had been taken when Govind graduated from Amritsar University. His turbaned head, with sleek moustache and confident eyes, stared out with a faint look of surprise, as though marvelling that he, the son of a simple farmer, could rise to such heights.

Govind had come to England to study, encouraged by Harold Chadwick, his English teacher back in India. He enrolled at London University to do a degree in law. He was urged to be someone; do something for his newly-independent country. But all these plans had been interrupted by the war. He had joined up along with all his fellow students and fought in Europe and North Africa.

So where was that hero now? Where was the soldier-scholar, whose garlanded image Jaspal had grown up with and admired every day. Where was the Sikh warrior, who had gone into the British army to help fight against the Nazis? When the war ended, and Govind didn't come home, they never for a moment disbelieved his letters, which told them first, that he had been wounded and was undergoing treatment, and then, that he was trying

45

to earn enough money in Britain, so that he could return to India and set up a business.

Jaspal remembered how his mother, Jhoti, had fretted. 'Why doesn't he come home? We need him here. We need him as a father to protect his family. Doesn't he know what is happening here?'

Surely Govind must have heard. The whole world knew that Britain had finally granted India the right to independence. But even before the British left, the troubles began. When part of India split away to become Pakistan, in the vast interchange of populations from one country to another, thousands were slaughtered. And in the Punjab, the Sikhs, who were neither Hindu nor Muslim, fought for their own identity – and some, for their own homeland too. How could Govind not know? Why did he not return to protect his family?

But what did Govind, their father, know of all this? It was ten years since he had left India, and it was as though he had never belonged there, never had a family there, no parents, brothers or sisters, no wife and two young children.

By the time he married Maeve O'Grady, he was another person altogether. He never talked about India to her; never told her about his other wife and children; and the more time went by, the less reason he saw to confess – especially after Beryl was born.

Then Jaspal and Marvinder turned up on his doorstep in England and, like a thrust of the wheel, his whole world revolved and his past life confronted him.

At first, Jaspal couldn't believe this was his father. He had no beard, no turban. He wasn't a scholar or a warrior, or anyone he could be proud of. Worst of all, Govind had betrayed them all; Jaspal, Marvinder and their mother, Jhoti.

Then they found out he was part of a criminal gang.

Bitterly, all Jaspal could hear was Mr O'Grady's words ringing in his ears, 'He's nothing but a spiv; a black-marketeer; a petty crook.'

'But he did save a man from the fire,' Jaspal had pleaded. 'The newspapers said he was a hero.'

'Just as well,' Mr O'Grady had snorted. 'Otherwise he would have gone to the gallows for murder.'

For that heroic act, they hoped his other crimes would be overlooked, but it was not to be. The wheels of justice turned, and Govind was convicted for black-marketeering.

'It's good that Ma never knew what Pa did in England,' Marvinder had whispered when their father was taken off to prison.

Govind held out his hands greedily, eager to clasp each one. Jaspal avoided his father's gaze and pulled away from Govind's grip as soon as he could. He flopped down in a chair, and turned it sideways on, looking deliberately bored.

Marvinder pulled her chair closer, but sat with lowered eyes. No matter what Govind had done, she couldn't hate him, and she wished she had magic powers, so that she could free him from his prison. She often imagined how she would help him to escape and they would all run away back to India. Then they would find her mother, Jhoti, and everything would be all right.

'How are you doing for money?' Govind asked Maeve. They sat facing each other across the table. They didn't touch; each kept their hands clasped together in front of them.

'We're managing,' she replied sullenly. 'I've got a job at Franklands Engineering. Gives me about fifteen bob a week; a pound, with overtime. Between Mum, Dad and the boys, we get by. We get Family Allowance too. They've agreed to give it for Jaspal and Marvinder, as well as for Beryl, and I've got ration books for them now. That friend of yours, Mr Chadwick, he found out about it all for us.'

'That's good.' Govind sighed with relief. 'How's Beryl?'

'She's fine.' Maeve fingered her wedding ring so that she didn't have to look at her husband. 'The children bring home these American food parcels from school. That helps,' she murmured.

Govind waited for more news of their child, but Maeve fell silent and went on twisting her ring round and round.

'I've got something for her.' Govind reached down to a brown paper bag at his feet and pulled out a stuffed elephant.

'That's nice!' Marvinder exclaimed with enthusiasm. It was patchworked together from different bits of material and stuffed. 'Isn't it nice, Maeve?'

'I made it in the workshops,' Govind said with weary pride. 'I'm halfway through a camel. It'll be ready next time you come. But I hope Beryl will like the elephant.' He stood it on the table for them to admire.

'It's lovely, isn't it, Maeve!' Marvinder persisted. 'Course Beryl will like it, won't she?'

Maeve nodded, giving it a cursory glance, but made no move to examine it. Marvinder picked it up. 'Look, *bhai!*' She showed the elephant to Jaspal. 'Isn't Pa clever to make this?'

'Why did you make an elephant?' queried Jaspal in a cold voice. 'They don't have elephants here or camels, except in zoos. You should have made a dog or a cat.'

'Shall I make you a dog or a cat?' asked Govind, trying to please.

Jaspal almost snorted with derision. 'Stuffed toys are for babies! Billy's father makes boats. He sails them in the park. He might let me make one,' added Jaspal cruelly.

'Who's Billy?' asked Govind quietly.

'My best friend,' said Jaspal. 'His dad might give me a job later in his workshop. He said I had all the makings of a carpenter. I can still remember everything old uncle taught me back in India.'

'Who was your best friend in India? You used to write to me about him. The son of that Muslim tailor, Khan, wasn't he?'

'Nazakhat,' said Marvinder, when she saw Jaspal purse his lips tightly 'Nazakhat and the Khans saved our lives. Without their help we would have been killed...' Her voice trembled as she remembered.

'Perhaps you should never have left Deri,' murmured Govind. 'Perhaps you should have stayed and taken your chances. Your friends, the Khans may have continued to protect you.'

'They're all dead,' stated Jaspal, flatly.

'Oh, Jaspal, how can you say that?' protested Marvinder. 'We don't know anything for sure.'

'I've read all about it in the papers. Millions have died, especially in the Punjab. Nazakhat must be dead. Ma, too. We would be dead if we'd stayed.' His voice was cold and emotionless. There was an uncomfortable pause. Then Govind changed the subject. 'Maeve says you're going to be sitting the eleven-plus. You could go to grammar school and maybe to university.' Govind leaned forward earnestly. 'You could do what I was meant to do, if you study hard.'

'Huh!' Jaspal snorted again and turned away, no longer interested in communicating with his father.

'What do you want to go putting ideas into his head like that for?' Maeve reproached him in a shrill voice. 'We're short enough of money as it is, what with you in here. The sooner he's out earning, the better – and her!' She indicated Marvinder. 'That Dr Silbermann's giving her ideas too, what with all this violin playing. I don't think it's healthy, all the time she spends down there.'

Govind looked at his daughter and sighed. In India, he would have been negotiating her dowry and arranging a marriage for her. She was exactly the same as Jhoti, her mother, when he married her.

'Perhaps when I get out, I'll take Marvi back to

India and get her marriage arranged. That would be the best.' He spoke with the sudden enthusiasm of a good idea.

'No, Pa, no!' Marvinder stared at her father in horror.

'I thought you wanted to go back.' He frowned.

'I do, I do. But I want to go back with you and Jaspal. I want to go home. I want to find out about Ma. I don't want to get married. No one here gets married so young.' Tears welled up in her eyes at the thought.

Maeve shrugged. 'Come off it, Govind, she's only thirteen, and she hasn't even started her monthlies. I was thinking maybe she could do a paper round.'

'I'd like a horse,' said Jhoti inside Marvinder's head. 'A bridegroom's horse, all decorated and ribboned.'

'Could you make a horse?' Marvinder asked her father, wiping her eyes on her sleeve. 'I'd like a horse.'

'Of course,' replied Govind. 'I'll make one for you by the next time you come. It doesn't take long.'

SIX

Who Will You Marry?

Marriage. The word; the thought of it, threw Marvinder into a state of dark imaginings. On the way home from prison, she left Jaspal alone at the front of the bus and joined Maeve at the back. She wanted to talk to her about it. But Maeve wasn't in the mood; she puffed on her cigarette, enveloping them both in a haze of blue smoke, and stared out of the dirt-streaked window. She looked shut away into her own thoughts and unwilling to be drawn out.

For a while, they just sat there in silence, occasionally lurching up against each other as the bus bumped or turned a corner.

Marvinder glanced up at her. She wanted to run a finger over that smooth, white skin, to know whether white skin felt the same as brown skin. Or was it cooler? More delicate? Would her brown finger bruise it in some way? Leave a mark or a smudge? She tried to slip her hand in Maeve's, which rested, ungloved on her lap. Maeve looked down at her, surprised, her green eyes looking as lost as pebbles falling through water.

'Maeve! Do you think my pa will make me marry?' Marvinder asked timidly.

Maeve drew her hand away and replaced her glove. 'How should I know,' she murmured vaguely. 'I suppose you lot have your own customs. But I wouldn't let no daughter of mine get married off while she's still a child. It's not right.'

'What did you mean about not having started my monthlies?' asked Marvinder.

'Oh . . .' Maeve looked embarrassed. 'You'll find out in due course. I expect me mum'll tell you,' and she turned her face away to look out of the window once more.

That night, Marvinder tried to speak to Jhoti about it. But like dreams, Jhoti had her own timing, and could not be summoned up at will.

'Is it as bad as all that?' asked Dr Silbermann, her friend in the basement below.

Marvinder went down with her violin almost every day after school. Down to a dim, dusty netherworld, smelling of glue and varnish. It was a planet made entirely of paper. Sheets of music, newspapers, clippings, and magazines covered every possible surface. They spread out, layer upon layer across the floor, or were piled into strange organic-like structures which always seemed about to topple over. There were books rising precariously in tall higgledy-piggledy towers, balanced along the mantelpiece like the distant skyline of some foreign city. The few bits of furniture that he owned – a bed, table, a chest of drawers, a couple of buried armchairs and his old grand piano, seemed only to be there to provide a surface for more books and music.

If anyone came to call, he would sweep a pile of papers to the floor revealing a battered armchair with its stuffing hanging out. Here, in a flurry of dust, his visitor would sit down.

Marvinder never saw him eat. His small gas cooker was always covered in tins of varnish and glue, and his sink never seemed free from jam jars stuffed with brushes, soaking in methylated spirits.

Above the sink hung a row of glistening violins in all shades of yellows and reds and golden browns, drying, after they had been freshly varnished and restored by him. He called them his children, and Marvinder knew that they were all he had left to love, since his own children had perished in the Nazi concentration camps.

But each day when she called, he would study her face, and know her mood and, today, he saw it was solemn and thoughtful. He looked kindly into her eyes and tweaked her chin. 'So? Has Chicken Licken heard that the sky's falling down?' he chuckled.

Marvinder laughed then nearly cried. She hastily took out her violin and began tuning it. When she had recovered herself a bit, she said, 'Do you think I'll be ready for my exam next summer?'

But what she was really saying inside herself was, 'My pa is thinking of taking me back to India to get me married. I don't want to get married. Mrs O'Grady says he won't make me. She said they'd all be against it. But if Pa says I must . . . I'll have to . . .'

'Of course you'll be ready. Why, you'd be ready next month if it were necessary,' Dr Silbermann replied reassuringly. 'You're not worrying about it, are you?'

'No, not really!'

'You're getting on like a house on fire,' smiled Dr Silbermann. 'By the time you've played in the festival and given the Chadwicks a recital, you'll be truly good and ready.'

'I was married at your age,' murmured Jhoti, *from inside her daughter's head. 'We all have to in the end.'*

'Why?' *asked Marvinder silently.*

'Because you do. That's what life is about.' Her *mother sighed. 'It's our duty.'*

'Were you happy?'

'Happy? Ah . . .' *Her mother faded.*

Dr Silbermann sat down at the piano and began to play the introduction of 'La Paloma'. The sun streamed through the low bay window, creating a cosmos of molecules, where millions of specks of dust floated like planets, and the old Doctor of Music himself seemed to disintegrate in the shafts of light.

The notes from the piano rocked like a boat. Marvinder made her entry, her bow lightly bobbing across the strings, short and long, breathing out the phrases like a human voice singing.

'I always think of the blue waters of the Mediterranean, when I hear this piece. I had never seen the sea before I went to Barcelona,' Dr Silbermann said dreamily, as they came to the end.

'Where's Barcelona?' asked Marvinder.

'It's in Spain, where the sun always shines. I went there once as a young man before the war. I gave a recital in a concert hall just off the main square. It was wonderful. We were so young and so hopeful. We thought music was the universal language. That all we had to do was play, and everyone would understand. We believed that music was the answer to all the ills of the world and that Barcelona was the most beautiful city in the universe. We were foolish. We thought that Beauty was Truth and Truth was Beauty.' He sighed at the memory. 'Perhaps one day, you'll go to Spain.'

'And give a recital?' asked Marvinder.

'Why not?' Dr Silbermann smiled brightly. Then, as he turned back to the keyboard, he played a soft chord and murmured again, 'Why not?'

When, later on upstairs over tea, Marvinder talked about going to Spain to give a concert, Michael and Patrick roared with laughter, and Mr O'Grady frowned disapprovingly.

'What's so funny?' Marvinder protested, blushing uncomfortably. 'Dr Silbermann says I might. He should know.'

'Dr Silbermann's soft in the head. It's the war what done it, and him losing all his family like that. Poor sod. I'm not blaming him, but you shouldn't go getting any fancy ideas, my girl,' said Mrs O'Grady.

'I think you should stop her going down there,' declared Mr O'Grady. 'It's bad for her.'

'Yeah, Dad's right,' agreed Michael. 'All this caterwauling she does. Where's it going to get her?'

Marvinder was outraged. The blood rushed angrily to her cheeks. Caterwauling? No one had ever referred to her violin-playing like that before.

'Hey!' Patrick teased her raucously. 'No need to go to Spain and upset the bulls, Marvinder. You'd get an appreciative audience down in the church-yard with all them cats.'

'Or how about the pub on a Saturday night? But none of that classical stuff, mind. You'd have to learn some Irish airs,' yelled Michael gleefully. 'I'll teach you "When Irish Eyes Are Smiling",' and he broke into the song with great panache.

'Fancy playing in the pub, Marvi?' yelled Patrick, slapping his brother on the back with the enjoyment of ganging up on Marvinder. 'Play us some jigs we can dance to!'

Marvinder got to her feet, with outraged tears streaming down her cheeks. 'I hate you, Patrick O'Grady, and you too, Michael,' she shouted.

'Hey, hey! Settle down, all of you,' bellowed Mrs O'Grady above the hubbub. 'Stop that silly non-sense, boys. Come on, Marvinder. They were only teasing. You know what boys are. You play like an angel. We all know that. Sit down, there's a good girl.'

Marvinder subsided back into her place, rubbing her nose along her sleeve and hiccuping with emo-tion. Kathleen leaned into her and patted her gently.

'Take no notice, Marvi. You know they're just stupid. All boys are stupid.'

'Who are you going to marry when you grow up?' Marvinder whispered in the darkness as, that night, she and Kathleen lay side by side in the bed they had to share.

Kathleen giggled softly. 'How should I know?'

'Don't your mum and dad have a boy in mind for you?'

'Course not! Anyway, I don't think I want to marry.'

'Why not?' cried Marvinder.

'It's too much work. All those babies and things. Look at Mum. Look how hard she has to work; all that scrubbing and cleaning and washing and cooking. I don't want to do that.'

'Maeve's only got one child. She doesn't work so hard,' remarked Marvinder.

'Yeah, I know. Father Macnally's always telling her off. He thinks she should have more by now. "It's your Catholic duty to have babies for Jesus," ' mimicked Kathleen. 'It would be just my luck to marry a man who gave me thirteen children like Mrs Hannagan. Can you imagine looking after thirteen children?'

'I thought you might marry Tommy Henderson. He likes you lots,' grinned Marvinder. 'You like him too, don't you?'

Kathleen blushed bright red. 'Don't be bloody daft. Anyhow, he's a Protestant. How about you? Who will you marry?'

'No one,' stated Marvinder categorically. 'No one. I'd hate to be married.'

Yet inside her, she knew the opposite was true. Only a few days ago, they had gone to the cinema to see the new Walt Disney film, *Snow White*. She thought it was the most beautiful, frightening and wonderful thing she had ever seen. When she had come out, blinking into the daylight, she felt she was Snow White. She understood Snow White's sadness at having lost her mother and how cruel it was to be hated and rejected by her stepmother; and how her father didn't seem to notice or care or try to defend her. Snow White longed to be loved and to have a home and happiness. Marvinder learned all the songs and sang them at school, while they waited in the dinner line. 'Some day my prince will come . . .'

'No one? Never?' asked Kathleen, pressing her.

'Well, maybe . . . someday,' said Marvinder.

SEVEN

To the Borders of Death

It is sometimes hard to believe that the sun which rises up and up like a blazing chariot into a vast, blue Indian sky, is the same pale sun, which seeps weakly through the hard, grey canopy of a sky in England; where its very scarcity gives the sun a value, and its fragility induces a sense of wonder.

It is even more difficult to realise that the Thames, which flows so broad and busy past Battersea, flanked by warehouses and walls and embankments, is the same river which starts life in a Gloucestershire field. The source bubbles fretfully up through the mole-humped grass, somewhere behind a pub called the Thames Head, and homes ambitiously across water meadows to become a stream. Then, after meandering amiably between marshy banks, trailing with willow, its reeds haunted by water rats and coots and piping moorhens, it gains in strength and power, until, by the time it leaves Lechlade, it is swiftly flowing like an unbridled horse, wandering wherever it wills: eastwards, and northwards, then doing a complete loop and dropping down southwards to Oxford, no sooner going this way, than it turns and goes that way; past Abingdon, Maidenhead, Windsor and

Richmond, finally heading for London, and beyond London, to the sea.

'I think that the River Thames joins up with the Ganges in India.'

Edith Chadwick was standing in the bay window of the living room, staring out at the river which they could see from their house in Richmond.

'Good heavens, Edith! How do you reach that conclusion?' exclaimed her mother with uneasy amusement.

'Well, the Thames flows out into the English Channel at Gravesend, and its waters become part of the sea. The Thames water could get swept round in the currents into the Atlantic and on into the Bay of Biscay and the Mediterranean. From there it joins the Suez canal and flows out into the Indian Ocean; and then . . .' she moved her finger in the air as if along a map, 'it meets up with the rivers of India which have been pouring down into the sea from the Himalayas, and they all become one. Aren't I right?' she challenged.

Dora laughed; it was a nervous high-pitched peal of laughter which sounded as though it could fragment into tears. 'Oh, Edith! You are a funny girl.' She tried to hug her daughter, but as usual, Edith's body went rigid as her mother's arms encircled her, and she pulled away.

'You see, Harold!' Dora cried desperately. 'She doesn't love me. My own daughter doesn't love me. Indeed, she hates me. I know she does.'

'No, Dora, stop!' cried Harold, desperately trying

to deflect his wife from another outburst of this sort. But hysteria overcame her with such suddenness these days, that he and Edith were left helpless.

'And why? Why?' Dora's voice rose with emotion. 'What have I ever done to you, Edith?' She turned to her pleadingly. 'Why do you treat me like your enemy? We used to be so close, you and I, until the twins were born. I know you hated Ralph and Grace, didn't you? Did you think we stopped loving you then? But they're dead now, and there's only you, and I don't blame you for their death. It's my fault and only mine, so why do you hate me now? Why can't you tell me, so that I can put it right?' She was sobbing pitifully. Great, heaving sounds wrenched through her body.

Edith backed away, her face expressionless. She turned to look out of the window where the sun glinted on the slow-moving body of the Thames. She wondered if she could carry on with the link she had made, so that the waters of the Thames somehow joined with the waters of that lake in the Punjab, where the twins had drowned. Perhaps even as she looked, their souls were floating by, and their voices calling out to her, 'Edie! Edie, wait for us!'

Harold came swiftly, and putting his arms round his wife, led her away to their bedroom. He gave her a sedative and sat with her till she calmed down and finally slept.

'Oh, God!' he whispered fiercely, as he caught a glimpse of his grey, anguished face in the dressing-table mirror. 'What has happened to us?'

Would they ever be a family again?

When he returned to the living room, Edith had barely moved from her position in the window. He stood next to her. He didn't touch her but, like her, looked out at the hard leaden surface of the river as it curved away. The variety of its moods and character never failed to fascinate; sometimes slowly moving, blue and benign, sometimes choppy and turbulent, sometimes just powerful and swiftly flowing. Today it looked indifferent.

'Perhaps you're right,' he murmured. 'I'd never thought of the Thames linking up with the Ganges, but it's a lovely idea. It makes me feel hopeful. I always did believe that we all belonged to each other in this world; that what happens in one part of the globe matters to the other parts.' He glanced sideways down at his daughter's face. Her dark, corn-coloured hair fell like a curtain, barely revealing the profile of her pale, high forehead and strong, straight nose. Her lips, though full and generous, were pursed tight, puckering her cheeks as she gazed impassively out of the window. She could have been made of stone. It was as though she had absented her body. Gone away. They had lost their twins, and it was as if they had lost Edith too. What could he do to bring her back? What would make her laugh again?

Unexpectedly, Edith asked, 'When are we going to see Jaspal and Marvinder again?' Harold reacted as joyfully as if she had hugged him. Of course, Jaspal and Marvinder! It was time they saw them again. Edith had always laughed a lot when she was with Marvinder.

'Whenever you like. Shall we ask Marvinder over for the day?' Harold cried eagerly. 'How about next Saturday?'

'Yes, but Jaspal must come too,' said Edith firmly.

'We'll play hide and seek,' announced Edith.

Jaspal and Marvinder stood silently side by side in the gloom of the second floor, where Edith's bedroom and playroom were.

They felt awkward and shabby and wished they weren't there. Mr Chadwick had called in at Whitworth Road after work one evening to invite them over to Richmond. Mrs O'Grady had been out pushing Beryl's old black pram round the streets, delivering laundry to her customers. If only she had been home when Mr Chadwick called, she might not have let this happen. She was suspicious of the Chadwicks. They belonged to a different class and a different world. They knew about Govind's past life in India, and it made her feel uneasy. She didn't want them interfering in their lives.

But only Maeve was home and, since she didn't care one way or the other, Maeve immediately agreed to Jaspal and Marvinder visiting the Chadwicks the following Saturday. Jaspal was furious. It meant missing *Flash Gordon* at the Saturday morning pictures. It was the highlight of his week, and then, afterwards, roaming round the streets with the gang, or train-spotting with Billy. When Harold Chadwick left, he raged at Maeve and declared that nothing would make him go. It would be boring being with girls – and especially that toffee-nosed Edith.

But when Mrs O'Grady came home, she said, 'Well, what's done's done. You'll have to go now, so you might as well stop fussing and make the best of it.'

Harold Chadwick and Edith were waiting at Richmond station to meet them. Harold welcomed them with jovial words, but Edith looked pale and restrained. It was raining hard, so Mr Chadwick had brought the car. They would have driven in silence, had not Mr Chadwick asked lots of questions such as, 'How is school?' 'Are the O'Gradys in good health?' and 'I'm so sorry it's raining, and we can't go boating. Oh well, there'll be plenty more opportunities . . .'

When they arrived at the house, Mr Chadwick called out to his wife as he opened the front door. 'Hello, darling! Dora! They're here!' There was no answer. 'I wonder where your mother is . . .' murmured Mr Chadwick. Edith shrugged. Everyone seemed awkward. Mr Chadwick took their coats and hung them up on a coatstand near the door.

Jaspal and Marvinder looked around, closely observing everything.

'It's more like a church than a house,' whispered Jaspal, looking at the black and white tiled floor in the hall passage, and the stained glass of deep reds, greens and yellows of the front door and the landing windows.

They went into the living-room. It was a living-room and nothing but a living-room, with sofas and armchairs and cushions and rugs, and pretty little coffee tables and a vase of flowers in the window near the wireless. A fire was blazing in the polished grate, reflecting and twinkling in the shiny brass fender.

Mr Chadwick again called out for his wife. Still she didn't answer. He tried to jolly up the atmosphere, cracking jokes and making suggestions about how they could pass the time with indoor play.

Edith said, 'I'll take them up to the top of the house. We'll play dressing up and maybe hide and seek.'

Jaspal threw his sister a look of disgust and, powerlessly, they followed Edith back out into the hall and upstairs.

How strangely quiet it was. Their feet made no sound on the rich, red stair carpet, and no voices emanated from any of the rooms. Everything smelt clean and aired and polished. They reached the first floor and padded past a walnut table with curved legs, above which hung a painting of English countryside with horses and golden fields.

They continued up another set of stairs and stopped on the landing of the second floor. Edith went to a far door and said, in a commanding voice, 'I am going up into the attic. Wait here until I call you.' Then she opened the door, and they caught a glimpse of a flight of steep wooden stairs rising up into the darkness above.

Jaspal stuck out his tongue furiously. 'Who does she think she is, that big fat snob, bossing us around like some princess. I want to go home right now. I hate it here. I hate Edith. I hate the Chadwicks. They're nothing but poshy, toshy, snotty-nosed idiots. I'm going!'

'Jaspal, no!' Marvinder grabbed his arm. But Jaspal shook her free. 'You can't stop me!' he cried and leapt down the short flight of stairs to the landing below. But it was only to come face to face with Dora Chadwick.

He stared at her, shocked to a standstill. 'Memsahib . . . Mrs Chadwick?'

She had seemed to float out of a room as if she were a stranger, lost in her own house. She carried a vase of flowers in her hand and vaguely held them up before her. 'Oh, Jaspal! It is Jaspal, isn't it?'

'Yes . . . it's me . . . Jaspal . . .' he replied haltingly.

Dora Chadwick gave a high laugh. 'You gave me a fright appearing out of the blue like that, as if you were a ghost . . . I keep thinking my little twins are playing hide and seek somewhere . . . I often hear them laughing you know . . . but I never see them . . .' Her voice trailed away. 'Are you having fun? Dear boy.' She put out a thin white hand and stroked his face. 'It's lovely to have you here. It's just like the old days, when you and my darling twins were such good friends . . . the gods saved you, Jaspal . . . they kept you on this earth . . .' Her eyes filled with tears. 'But my twins, they loved my twins too much and took them away. But they aren't far away, you know. Just playing hide and seek. Will you play hide and seek too?'

Jaspal recoiled from her touch, and slowly,

slowly, retreated back upstairs again, to where Marvinder was leaning over the banisters with worried eyes.

'Cooeee!' Mrs Chadwick cocked her head on one side and called up to them in a coy little voice. 'I see you!' She waved her hand childishly. 'Are you playing nicely with Edith?'

'Yes, Mrs Chadwick,' Marvinder replied reassuringly.

'*Are you going to play in the palace, Marvi?*' asked Jhoti.

'*No, Ma, we are in Edith's house in England. It is a big, tall dark house, with many rooms and stairs. We are going to play dressing up and maybe some hide and seek.*'

'*I am hiding too, Marvi. Tell Jaspal to come and find me . . .*'

'Ma!' Marvinder cried, 'Where are you?'

'There's good little children,' sighed Dora Chadwick. 'Don't forget to include the twins, will you? They do so hate being left out,' and nodding vaguely at them, she wandered off out of their sight.

Jaspal tapped the side of his head. 'She's mad!'

'You can come up now!' Edith called imperiously from above.

'We can go up now,' mimicked Jaspal with a cruel leer.

'Hush, *bhai!*' Marvinder gave him a kick. 'Behave yourself.' She gripped his arm and went to the bottom of the stairs.

'You go first,' she murmured, pushing her brother in front of her.

'No, you!' he hissed, ducking behind his sister.

'Coward!' jeered Marvinder, with soft vehemence. She hung back.

'Go on!' Jaspal pushed her in the small of her back.

'I said, you can come up now,' repeated Edith impatiently.

'Coming!' called Marvinder, querulously and began to mount the steps, pleased to note that Jaspal followed very closely, only one tread behind.

When they reached the top of the steps, they found they had left behind all traces of daylight, and were staring into complete darkness.

'Where are you?' asked Marvinder in a small voice. 'Are you hiding?'

Suddenly a sharp narrow beam of light flashed on and lit up a face. It seemed to rise above them, disembodied; grotesque; with deep hollows for eyes and sharp long shadows elongating the cheekbones, making it look more like a skull than a face. Jaspal and Marvinder gasped with surprise. Edith was standing on a chair near a small round table. She had dressed up in long flowing robes, and stood with her arms outstretched like a priestess. Then they saw the torch, balanced on end on the table, throwing the light upwards on to her face.

'You have entered into the fifth circle, the zone between this world and the next. Draw near, and sit down at the table,' Edith intoned.

'What are we playing?' asked Marvinder nervously. There was a flurry and rustling in the darkness. Edith used her torch to guide her down from the table to a chair and then on to the floor. Holding up the beam of light, she beckoned them over. 'Come and sit at the table.' She indicated three empty chairs and sat down in one of them.

'Are we playing dressing up?' Marvinder asked, straining her eyes into the darkness. 'Are there some clothes for Jaspal and me?'

'In a while. Sit here first. Mother likes me to play with Ralph and Grace, so we have to call them.'

Jaspal sat down. He didn't say a word. Marvinder could see his eyes gleaming in the darkness. She felt uneasy. She touched her brother's arm. 'Jaspal?'

He didn't answer, but stared straight ahead, waiting.

Marvinder sat down slowly, still looking at her brother. But he wouldn't look at her. 'What are you going to do, Edith?' she asked warily.

'Concentrate. We're all going to concentrate,' said Edith. 'We must all think hard about Ralph and Grace, and tell them to come and play with us. I want to talk to them. I've been trying for ages, but I can't do it by myself. You are the only other people who knew the twins, and Jaspal was with them when they died. They might come to him.'

She leaned forward, rested her arms on the table and spread out her fingers. 'We must touch fingers, and make a complete circle,' she instructed.

Jaspal was eager. He obeyed immediately and spread out his fingers, so that his two thumbs touched each other and one little finger touched Edith's.

70

Marvinder kept her hands tightly clenched in her lap.

'Marvi!' Jaspal turned and looked at her, and his look commanded her to do the same.

With a disparaging shrug, Marvinder put her hands on the table and stretched her fingers out to touch Jaspal's and Edith's.

Edith sighed with satisfaction, then she said, 'We must close our eyes and breathe in and out together very slowly, and we must concentrate on Ralph and Grace. Are you ready? Eyes closed,' commanded Edith.

Edith and Jaspal closed their eyes and began breathing in and out in unison. Marvinder didn't. She sat wide-eyed and anxious. She knew some of the women in the village in India used to invoke the spirits. It was dangerous. Terrible things could happen. People were known to lose their minds.

Edith opened one eye and saw that Marvinder's eyes weren't closed. 'Marvi, close your eyes. We can't do it without you. Don't you want to contact Ralph and Grace?'

'Edith, it's dangerous. We shouldn't do this,' whispered Marvinder tremulously. 'Please stop.'

'Jaspal wants to go on, don't you, Jaspal?' Edith spoke with low intensity. 'Jaspal went to the very borders of death, didn't you, Jaspal? You went with Ralph and Grace. What happened, Jaspal? Did you cross over? Did you go with them a little way? What was it like? I want to know. What is it like to die?'

Jaspal groaned. His fingers quivered as if a

current ran through them. He breathed in and out, with sharp intense sounds.

'Marvi! Shut your eyes. Help us,' begged Edith. 'Jaspal is already on his way. Please, Marvi! You can't stop now.'

Reluctantly, Marvinder closed her eyes. She could feel the tip of Jaspal's finger throbbing against hers. He was murmuring, 'Rani! I came with Rani!'

Rani was the water buffalo Jaspal used to look after when he was six years old. He had come that afternoon, riding on her back across the fields, heading for the lake at the abandoned palace, where Rani could go into the water and have a good wallow.

'Edie! Marvi! Wait for us!' The twins' voices floated through the air, pleading in vain, while Edith and Marvinder had cycled off to play at the palace and left them behind.

'We shouldn't have left them. It's our fault,' stuttered Marvinder as the memories rushed back.

Jaspal's finger quivered. 'Come and ride on Rani's back,' cried Jaspal. 'We can get to the palace across the fields. Rani can carry you. Come on! There's plenty of room.'

They felt like gods, riding across the fields that day. The twins all golden-skinned and hair like reaped corn, and Jaspal, black as Shiva, sitting between Rani's horns, urging her on with his willow stick.

'We came to the lake, and wanted to cross the water to the island in the middle, where the rajahs used to sit and fish. There was a boat lying at the water's edge.' Jaspal's voice seemed to vibrate in the darkness. He paused. There was silence, except for their breathing.

'We saw you,' said Edith, softly. 'Marvi and I were on the palace roof and we saw everything. Grace got into the boat first, and you and Ralph pushed it out and then had such a struggle to get inside. We laughed, didn't we, Marvi?'

'No, Jaspal no!' Marvinder was trembling as she relived that day. 'Can't we stop them? Please, Edith, let's stop them.'

'We managed to get in,' said Jaspal, 'Even though we were laughing so hard. Grace said, "There's water in the boat, it's got into my sandals." "Look at me," cried Ralph, "I'm completely soaked." There was only one oar. Ralph took it because he was the biggest. He tried to row, but it was hard. Grace and I were leaning over the side using our hands.'

'We saw you, we saw you!' cried Edith.

'At first, the boat moved. It floated out into the middle of the lake. Grace kept saying, "There's water in the boat. It's getting higher." We didn't take any notice, but she cupped her hands and tried to scoop it out. At last we saw she was right. The boat was filling up with water. Ralph dropped the oar, and all of us just tried to chuck the water out. But it was no use. The water was rushing in – and the next thing . . . the next thing . . . was the boat was sinking beneath our feet . . .' Jaspal was whimpering and gasping . . . as if his lungs were filling with water.

Marvinder snatched her hands away from the table. 'Stop,' she pleaded. 'Stop! This is a bad game.'

But Edith grabbed her wrists and forced Marvinder's hands back on to the table. 'This isn't a game. I want to know!' she cried. 'I want to know what it was like.'

'I had my eyes open, when I went down.' Jaspal was speaking more calmly now. 'Everything was green. The twins had become green. Their yellow hair floated all around them like long green grass. Their arms and legs reached out, as if trying to find something to cling on to. Their eyes were open, their mouths were open. We were calling for help. We were dropping down, down, down. Then everything went dark. There was a rushing sound in my ears . . . I . . .'

Marvinder felt the pressure of Edith's fingers pressing into her own. 'I was always wishing that they would go away. I used to pray for them to die,' Edith whispered harshly. 'What happened next, Jaspal? What is it like to die?'

They heard screaming. Marvinder thought it was the twins as they drowned, but then she realised it came from behind them. Dora Chadwick was standing at the top of the stairs, her mouth wide open.

EIGHT

The Wild Child

The wild child crouched by the shore of the lake.

The boys were afraid of it. They had a meeting and discussed what they should do. One Eye was all for driving it away. A group of other boys agreed. They leapt to their feet and were keen to set to immediately with sticks and stones.

But Bublu cried, 'Wait!'

'Why wait?' One Eye challenged him. One Eye always snatched any opportunity he could to oppose Bublu.

'Yeah! Why wait?' There was a chorus of agreement from some of the others. There was nothing they liked better than an excuse for a fight or action. 'Let's go for that animal.'

'We don't know who it is or what it is. It came with the horse. In the bazaar, they said the horse was a portent; an omen . . .' Even as Bublu spoke the words, they sounded ridiculous and his voice died away uncertainly.

But it had an effect. They all looked over to the water's edge, where the child crouched, its eyes glinting through the scraggle of hair. They hated it, because it wouldn't respond – either to come closer and be a part of them, or retreat and escape their hostility. It was just there; a presence which they couldn't explain or understand.

Ever since the horse had come some nights ago and left it on the terrace, the child had done nothing except glower silently at them, always from a distance.

Bublu had tried to make contact, approaching it slowly with outstretched hand as one would approach a stray cat. But each time, the child retreated on two legs, or on all fours, arching its back, spitting and hissing.

They called it Jungli – the wild one.

Every morning, it was there when they woke up, and there every night when they finally slumped into exhausted sleep. It seemed to have them under constant surveillance; spying on them, watching them like a guard or a witch's familiar.

There had been times in the middle of the night, when a boy had awoken to hear scuffling and was sure that Jungli was in there with them, skulking in the darkness. Panicky cries of alarm had led to chaos and pandemonium and left the boys sleepless with terror.

One Eye picked up a stone and chucked it so hard that it pitted the dust in front of the creature. 'It gives me the creeps! How do we know it's not some vampire? It's a wonder it hasn't sucked our blood in the night.'

This thought aroused an explosion of fears in the group, and many of the boys again urged action. 'Yeah! It can't be human. If it is, then it's a freak! Get rid of it, I say!' And some of the others hurled handfuls of dust and pebbles at the creature, till it lolloped away along the shore.

Something had to be done, there was no question. It was upsetting the group and causing divisions.

'I'll see if I can find out something in the bazaar. All right?' declared Bublu more authoritatively. 'Old Sharma might know about these things. We don't want to risk bringing trouble down on ourselves. So just wait, eh? One more day.'

There was a surly murmur of agreement, though One Eye's lot seemed very reluctant.

When Bublu had gone, One Eye beckoned the others round. Sparrow hung among the pillars, staying out of sight. He was considered too small to bother about anyway.

'We should at least try and catch it,' said One Eye. 'Then we can decide what to do with it.'

'Huh! And who's going to do that, may I ask? Haven't we tried catching it already? No one can get near it,' retorted one of the boys.

'We just haven't thought of a plan that's clever enough,' argued One Eye. 'We've been thinking of it as a human instead of as a wild animal. We have to think like hunters and trappers. Look! What if we lure it into the palace. We could leave some food in the courtyard, and then leave a trail of food leading into the inner chamber. There's a door to that room. If we can get it inside, we can slam the door, and then it'll be our prisoner. My pa once caught a cheetah like that.'

'Tch!' snorted Kite scornfully. 'Then what do we

do? Who's going to go in and tie him up without getting their eyes scratched out, eh?'

'Idiot! Think I'm stupid? Why, then we all crowd round the door with our rope. When we open the door it's bound to come out and that's when we jump on it and tie it up. After all, it's hardly bigger than a monkey. I tell you, that Bublu is nothing. He's a fool. He's gone soft. It's time you listened to me. Let's show him!'

'Yeah! Let's!' agreed a number of boys, though others scowled suspiciously, and were uneasy at doing anything behind their leader's back. However, they were outnumbered, and so reluctantly agreed to co-operate with One Eye's plan. Only Sparrow kept clear, deciding to climb higher and higher to the upper terraces of the palace, his heart thumping with fear and foreboding. As soon as he could, he would get away and warn Bublu.

He could see the boys circled together. They pulled out whatever old bits of chapatti and sweets they had secreted about themselves and handed it all over to One Eye.

As planned, One Eye placed a small amount towards the centre of the courtyard, and then made a tantalising trail of morsels into the inner room.

The boys dispersed, choosing a number of vantage points round about, from which they could observe the courtyard and watch for the creature.

They waited and, for once, felt cheerful because they were on the attack. They no longer cared what Bublu was doing. This time they were taking the initiative and they waited eagerly for the moment of action. One Eye knew this was his opportunity to get the leadership of the group. If they caught the creature, Bublu would be discredited.

It was a long wait. The sun rose hot and high. Some of the boys dozed off. Sparrow tried to sidle away. He wanted to warn Bublu. But One Eye saw him, and with a silent but fierce gesture, ordered him back. Sparrow shrank into the shadows, ashamed at being so helpless. The morning slid silently into afternoon.

A sudden sharp cawing of a crow jerked them all awake. One Eye glared angrily as the black, shining bird hopped boldly over to the food in the courtyard. One Eye was just wondering whether to scare it away with a stone when, suddenly, into the doorway sprang the child. The crow pounced on a piece of chapatti. The child leapt forward with a desperate grunt, trying to snatch it back. But it was too late. The crow flapped away, the chapatti held firmly in its beak. The child scampered forward and thrust its face to the ground like an animal.

All eyes watched in fascination, willing it on into the trap. The child paused for a moment and looked up; it seemed to listen, cocking its head this way, then that. Then suddenly, its mouth went down again, hungrily, and it carried on eating, unaware that it was being drawn nearer and nearer towards the inner room. One Eye had positioned himself on the upper, screened, inner balcony. He was as close as he could get to the door without being seen. He waited, straining his eyes through the marble lacery. Its fine, intricate shadow fell upon the child as it shuffled, nose to the ground immediately beneath him. One Eye poised on tiptoe, until the child had followed the crumbs into the darkness of the room, then, lithe as a lizard, he slithered down a sapling and flinging himself on to the door, slammed it shut. There was one brief, terrible shriek from within – then silence.

With a roar of triumph, all the other boys emerged from their hiding places and dashed up to the door. They hammered it and yelled ecstatically for several minutes. It was at that moment Sparrow fled.

They waited a long time. They pressed their ears to the door, listening for any sound.

'What is it doing?'

'Could it have found a way to escape?'

'Of course not, it's a windowless room, and only this one door.'

'What do we do now, then?'

'How long do we wait?'

'Will it come out, or must we frighten it out?'

One Eye said, 'Form a tight circle round the door. You, Koil and Swan, hold this sheet between you. Vulture and I will have the rope ready. Fever, when I give the word, you open the door. Jungli will rush straight into the sheet and you will drag it to the ground. Then Fever and I will truss it up and it will be ours!'

So they formed a circle and held out the sheet.

One Eye and Vulture each had an end of rope. They waited and listened again.

'I hope it's still in there!' whispered Koil.

'Course it is,' sneered One Eye. 'All right. Ready, Fever?' Fever nodded. 'NOW!' yelled One Eye.

Fever flung open the door.

Nothing happened.

They stood there, their bodies braced for impact, ready to pounce on their victim – but – nothing. Nothing happened.

'Arreh? What now? Where's the devil gone?'

'Perhaps it's invisible!'

'Yeah! Like a ghost. It probably walked out through the walls.'

'Bublu was right! It's a demon! We shouldn't have tried to catch it,' stammered Swan, hysterically.

'What nonsense you all speak!' snorted One Eye. He picked up a stone and threw it inside. Its fall echoed eerily. Nothing. One Eye moved right up to the entrance.

'One Eye, no!' pleaded Koil.

One Eye peered into the darkness. Nothing. He made a noose and stepped inside, whirling the end of his rope round and round in front of him.

Everyone held their breath. Time seemed to hang like a spider in the doorway; silent on the end of its thread – motionless – waiting . . .

When from out of the room, shot like a cannon-ball, a body hurtled into the sheet with such silent impact that the boys tumbled to the ground, winded and speechless. The spider swayed violently with the force. Only One Eye made any sound. He

81

emerged, waving his empty noose and bellowing, 'Catch it, catch it, you blithering idiots!' But the creature had gone.

When Bublu returned, One Eye was sitting a little apart from a disconsolate and shame-faced group.

They wouldn't get much to eat that evening, having used most of what they had trying to trap the wild child.

Listlessly, they collected wood for the evening fire and prepared for a cold and hungry night. A low howl drew their attention to the shore. Jungli was back. Watching them. Mocking.

Bublu slipped away and climbed the stone steps which took him up and up to the highest tier of the palace. From here, he could walk round and look in all directions – to the distant Himalayas in the north, floating like heaven, ethereal, pink and white as opals in the evening light; to the south, where the long white road ran like a gleaming ribbon past All Souls' Church; past the Chadwicks' deserted bungalow and on into the dusty twilight, as if the low, earthy village where his friend Jaspal had lived, was not worth even a glance. Then he faced Mecca to the west. He watched the huge orange sun slipping inch by inch behind the oblong shape of the Hindu temple. He should have been able to see the mosque, and hear the evening call to prayer echoing round the fields, but the mosque had been destroyed in the troubles and all Muslims, but a few orphans and old or tormented people, murdered or fled.

As if to remind himself who he was, Bublu lifted his arms up above his head and called out softly, 'My name is Nazakhat Khan! There is no god but God and Muhammad is his prophet.' Then he knelt down and bent forward till his head touched the ground. 'Allah Akbar!'

When he got to his feet and looked eastwards towards the lake, he saw the teacher. He had got used to seeing him at this time of day. There was something reassuring in the fact that both of them had a routine – the teacher, his daily walk by the lake with book in hand, and Bublu, his regular evening prayer up on the palace roof.

'One day,' Bublu thought to himself, 'I'll talk to him. Remind him who I am. But not yet. It's too soon to trust anyone.'

NINE

The Catch

Over the next few days, One Eye skulked off on his own. He didn't tell anyone, but he had formulated another plan. He made himself a catapult. He pretended to go off when the others did, but secretly circled round and returned to the palace. He had a hunch that the wild child would come back. He was sure of it. Nothing so far had scared it away. He would get to it if it was the last thing he did. He ground his teeth with vengeful determination, still smarting from the humiliation of the day before.

He found a tree, spreading chaotically in a tangle of climbers and creepers. He detected the very vantage point he was looking for – a leafy, forked branch halfway up, where he could sit comfortably for a few hours with a good view of both the palace and the lake shore.

His pockets were stuffed with sizeable stones, and he lay back along the length of the branch admiring the weapon he had made. Some time back, he had picked up a broken rubber fan belt from a burnt-out garage, and kept it, in case it came in useful for something. What could be better? He flexed it from the wooden Y-shaped chunky twig he had selected. It felt good. He took one of his stones, fitted it to the band and aimed at a crow who perched on a branch just above him. He flexed the rubber, pulling it back and back, then let go. He laughed out loud with satisfaction, as the stone hurtled through the air and struck the bird's wing. With a loud cry, it flapped in pain, and flew off low, leaving a black feather to spiral slowly down to the ground. So he passed the day, dozing, or catapulting off a few small stones at nothing in particular and waiting.

The sun was halfway down to dusk when he saw the wild child. It came loping along the shore, occasionally kicking at the water to create a spray which rose and fell like a handful of diamonds tossed into the air. The child obviously thought it was alone, for every now and then it gave strange whooping cries of pleasure.

The wild child was coming closer now. One Eye got up slowly, and with his bare toes outspread, balanced himself against the trunk of the tree. With his fingers, he rummaged in his pocket and selected a big, sharp stone. Taking it out, he fitted it to the catapult, his eyes barely leaving their target for a moment. The child had its back to the shore, and was now loping along the track towards him. One Eye aimed. He pulled back the rubber belt . . . waited till the child was within range . . . and let go. Like a bullet fired from a gun, the stone struck the child's head.

The wild child gave one shriek and fell to the ground.

'Bullseye!' yelled One Eye, with the triumph of a

hunter. He slithered down the tree and raced over to the unconscious creature. He danced round it hollering, 'Yeah, yeah! I did it!' He raced over to the palace and back again, whooping with his achievement.

His yells brought the others dashing through the undergrowth.

'Look what I did!' shouted One Eye, gleefully waving his catapult around his head.

The boys gave a cheer of admiration. They joined One Eye, stamping and circling round the crumpled body. Bublu appeared. The boys saw him and shouted, 'See! One Eye did it! We won't be bothered by this wretch any more!'

One Eye walked slowly forward to greet his rival, then stopped, arrogantly putting his hands on his hips. 'That's the way to deal with wild animals,' he announced.

At first, a murmur of agreement swept round the boys, but was cut short as they saw Bublu's furious face.

'You blithering idiot! You murderer! You son of a pig! What the hell did you go and do that for?' raged Bublu.

'Because he was bad luck. You said so yourself. He was annoying us all. You should be pleased, I've done you all a favour.'

'You've killed him, you oaf! That's what you've done!' Bublu looked down in horror at the blood gushing from a deep wound on the side of the child's head.

'Yeah, I did what you were too feeble and cowardly to do. I've put the creature out of action. You're nothing but an old woman!' taunted One Eye.

With a bellow of fury, Bublu flung himself on top of One Eye, with fists pummelling and legs kicking. Their grunts and yells brought other boys running, and soon they had circled the warring pair.

Bublu could hear some boys were rooting for One Eye, and he knew this was another fight for the leadership. But Sparrow's shrill voice pierced through the rest as he begged Bublu to 'Get him! Get him! Go on, Bublu! Knock him out.'

Bublu turned his shoulder to One Eye, and with a massive thrust pushed him to the ground. Bublu rolled on top of him; the boys struggled, and One Eye kicked out for all he was worth sending Bublu crashing backwards, dazed and bleeding. One Eye grabbed a large stone and rushed forward. Sparrow shrieked in horror as he saw One Eye raise the stone, ready to crash it down on Bublu.

'Oh no, you don't' bellowed a man's voice. The schoolteacher strode up behind One Eye, and grabbing both arms forced them behind his back as the stone fell to the ground. One Eye wriggled fiercely and kicked out with all his might. The teacher's grip loosened with pain and in that moment, the boy wrenched himself free and fled.

The others backed away warily. Who else might come? They looked around fearfully then shrank into the undergrowth.

Bublu got to his feet. Sparrow clung to him, whimpering quietly.

'Nazakhat, is it you?' The teacher frowned.

Bublu grabbed Sparrow round the waist and with a despairing shake of his head, stumbled away.

TEN

The Paper Round

It would be April before Marvinder realised that England could have long days of continuous sunshine.

It had seemed to be a land without colour – except the hard city colours of despair; hard grey, dull brown and dingy green. A country which had forgotten about the earth beneath its feet, or that somewhere beyond those leaden clouds, blazed a sun in a vast expanse of brilliant blue – as blue as Kathleen's eyes.

Then one day, Mrs O'Grady allowed the girls to toss aside the hated grey knee-length socks, with their useless bits of elasticated garters, and put on stiff, white ankle socks. As Marvinder hadn't yet got any, she borrowed Kathleen's only other pair.

Marvinder marvelled at the change. Although she instantly felt the chill on her bare skin, she had the airy sensation of having shed a load. She felt so light and free, she thought she would float away. This is how the moth must feel when it has broken out of its cocoon, or the snake, when it has dropped its old skin; a kind of rebirth, and with it, a soaring liberty; a contact with nature, like the bird with the sky or the fish with the ocean. For the first time, England was beautiful.

That day, Marvinder walked swiftly to school, sometimes breaking into a run, as though to increase the feel of the wind on her bare legs; and Kathleen had to run to keep up, shouting, 'What's the hurry?'

That day she was aware of nature bursting through; asserting itself, so that even the bomb-sites were transformed into wild gardens of tall grasses, long-limbed saplings and unruly flowers.

In the dinner hall, Marvinder couldn't help singing a song she had learned from the wireless, while the children waited in line, holding out their plates to get dollops of hot food from the dinner ladies.

'Though April showers may come your way,' she sang in a high, sweet voice.

Everyone nodded and smiled. It seemed to put them in a good mood.

'Do you remember April back home?' asked Jhoti.

She sometimes chose the most inconvenient moment to start talking to her daughter. Marvinder was sitting in class, attempting to concentrate on a history lesson about Elizabeth I, and trying not to let her eyes drift to the sight of the beech tree outside bursting into leaf.

The dreaded Mrs Humphreys of the red-rimmed spectacles and the sharp long fingernails, who was so adept with the ruler if a child misbehaved, was writing dates on the blackboard. Any minute now she would turn round and, like pointing a gun, aim a question at one of them.

'*Do you remember, Marvi?*' *Jhoti repeated, from inside her daughter's head.*

'*Yes, Ma. I remember,*' *murmured Marvinder, trying to concentrate on her history.*

'*It was always the best time, the harvest season in the Punjab,*' *her mother continued dreamily.*

All through February and March, the wheat crops would have been growing and ripening, and now, just before the full searing heat of May, the bullock carts would be creaking in endless convoy, going to and fro from the fields, laden as high as houses, with sheaves of wheat.

Marvinder gazed hopelessly out of the window. She felt as if her brain was being torn in all directions. Mrs Humphreys was hammering on about Elizabethan England; her mother's voice breathed inside her head, reminding her of home; and all the time, Marvinder's thoughts were tumbling with confusion. She wanted to go home; she wanted more than anything to go home; for things to be as they were and to be with her mother back in their own village once more. She had been dreaming about it, planning for it ever since she and Jaspal had arrived in England. She had even got a paper round to earn some money to put towards the boat fares. She and Kathleen were starting next Monday.

But all that had been blighted by her father saying, 'When I get out, I'll take Marvi back to India and get her marriage arranged,' and Marvinder had felt cast into an unfathomable darkness.

'Marvinder!'

Marvinder jerked with shock as her name was rasped across the classroom.

'Repeat what I just told you.' Mrs Humphreys' dark eyes sneered at her from behind those large, red-rimmed spectacles.

Marvinder looked around her desperately. Everyone was staring at her. Some sniggering with glee at her discomfort, others, like Kathleen and Josephine, were trying to mouth an answer to her, but she couldn't understand what they were saying.

'*When are you coming home, Marvi?*' *Jhoti asked her.*

'Soon, Ma. As soon as I can raise the money,' cried Marvinder, distracted and speaking out loud in Punjabi.

The whole classroom screamed with shocked pleasure at her insolence.

Mrs Humphreys seemed to grow taller and taller with rage, as she came out from behind her desk with ruler in hand. The red of her spectacles seemed as though they dripped with blood. The class subsided into an awesome hush as, with one finger, she prodded the space before her and summoned Marvinder.

Marvinder slid out from behind her desk and made her way down the aisle to the front. Fingers tugged her gymslip and feet thrust out to trip her up. Mrs Humphreys took up the wooden ruler as Marvinder stood before her. The teacher circled round her with silent fury then, pushing the girl's head forward, forced her into a bending position.

Even the strongest of them winced as the ruler swiped through the air across the backs of Marvinder's bare legs. Six strokes and not a word spoken.

Later, half the school came to examine the red weals on her skin and to hear about her insolence and heroism.

'Don't you feel pain like us?' asked Percy Gibson. 'My dad was in the army in India, and he told me about people who sleep on beds of nails and walk on burning coals and don't feel pain. Could you do that, Marvi?'

Kathleen and Josephine rescued her, linking their arms through hers and dragging her away.

'Of course she feels pain!' shouted Kathleen, who had seen the tears beginning to rise into her friend's eyes. 'She's just not a crybaby like some people we know!'

The alarm clock screamed briefly and was silenced by the experienced hand of Mrs O'Grady. It was Monday. The first day of doing the paper round.

Marvinder woke with the shock of Mrs O'Grady pulling back the blankets. Next to her, Kathleen gasped a protest! 'Hey, Ma! Don't!' she pleaded, as the chill air struck her sleep-warmed body.

But Mrs O'Grady had already moved on. They heard her fumbling for matches in the hall, and then after two rasping attempts at striking a match, heard the gaslight splutter into life. The grubby yellow beam was just sufficient for them to dress by.

'Don't you go pulling those blankets up again,'

she chided them, as Kathleen's hand fumbled down the bed. 'Up now!'

They heard a tap being turned on and a kettle filled; then again, the striking of a match and the pop of gas being ignited as she put the kettle on a ring to boil. Kathleen's hand found the edge of the blanket and pulled it up over them both. They slid back into sleep.

Mrs O'Grady returned. The girls had disappeared under the bedclothes.

'Come on,' she hissed firmly, once more stripping them bare. 'I'll only do this once to make sure you get up today, but tomorrow, you're on your own. I'll wake you and leave you to sort yourselves out. I don't have time to rush back and forth. After that, it's up to you. If you're going to do this job, then you've got to get up and see to yourselves.'

They got up. It was cold. It was horrible. They wished they weren't doing it. Marvinder was no longer sure why she was doing it.

'Must I marry if I go home? Must I?' The question rattled in her brain over and over again, but there was really no one to answer her. Mrs O'Grady only shrugged and said, 'Well, I suppose if that's your custom, you'll do as your father wishes.'

Once out in the grey, dawn streets, it was exciting. They felt special, almost privileged, as if they had been let into the secret of another world, of those who worked when others slept.

They saw people who moved like risen saints, gliding silently through dark, empty streets; walking, or on bicycles. It was the hour before the first

94

bus or the first underground train; the hour when milkmen cycle to their depots and the grooms wake up the giant Shire horses in the Express Dairy. They polish their blackened leather harnesses with the gleaming brass emblems, and link them to the milk carts loaded like snow, with cold white bottles; there are the quarter-pints and half-pints and whole pints, and jars of cream, all tinkling in their crates as the huge horses grate their hooves restlessly on the wet cobbles, and snort white steam into the chilled air.

Marvinder and Kathleen presented themselves at Fred Bingham's Newsagent at six o'clock prompt. He had just finished sorting out all the papers; the *Daily Mirror*, the *Daily Mail*, the *Express* and *News Chronicle*; the *Telegraph* and *The Times* – those were for the posh people – and the weekly magazines and the comics; ('Mind you don't go wasting time reading comics on the round!') and now the girls went into the back of the shop, where they had to help him allocate the right ones to the right names and addresses and transfer them to the large canvas shoulder bags.

Fred Bingham squinted at them over his spectacles, his pitted, drink-rotted skin was florid with his exertions. He stood too close to them and spoke into their faces so that they smelt his unwashed body; they recoiled in order not to breathe in his breath, reeking of tobacco and last night's beer.

'You're on trial,' he growled. 'One complaint, and you're off the job, do you hear? I've plenty of nippers would give their ears to have this job. I don't need you. If you can't do it properly, there are others. I told Kenny to stick around.' He indicated a boy who was slumped on the floor in a corner reading a comic. 'But only today, to show you the ropes. So you'd better pay attention. Here, you take this one.' He pushed a full bag over to Kathy and then elbowed her out of the back room.

He prodded the boy with his foot. 'Go on, Kenny. Scram!' The slow way the boy got to his feet was almost insolent and, tossing the comic on the table, he strolled behind Kathy to the front of the shop.

Marvinder went to follow, but Mr Bingham blocked her way. 'Just a moment, you. What did you say your name was?' He was standing close again. Marvinder backed away, but found herself pinned against a table. He leaned over her as if to reach for something, and pressed the full weight of his body up against hers. 'Your name, again?' he said softly. 'I need help with foreign names.' His face came down almost on top of hers.

'Marvinder!' she managed to gasp and, with a soft cry, slid to the floor and clambered out between his legs. 'Kathy?' she called out shakily. 'Kathy!'

Kathy appeared, the newspaper bag slung across her shoulders. 'I can manage this fine,' she said, smiling with pride.

Fred Bingham, his face looking red and annoyed, tossed out a second bag bulging with papers. 'You take this one,' he said to Marvinder without looking at her.

Keeping Kathy between her and him, Marvinder

reached out and dragged the bag towards her, then stumbled out of the shop.

'Get weaving, and be back by seven-thirty,' snarled Mr. Bingham. 'Ken here will show you the route today, but only today. So be sharp.'

'You all right?' questioned Kathy, noticing that Marvinder's earlier enthusiasm for the job had drained away.

'I'm all right,' answered Marvi shortly, and walked on in silence.

Ken was a small, thin-faced lad, with lank dark hair falling into his eyes. He smirked at them and set off striding, knowing full well they'd have difficulty keeping up.

'Oi! Kenny! Slow down, for God's sake!' moaned Kathleen, staggering under the weight of the bag.

But he didn't slow down till they reached Larkhall Rise. Then he waited, in a bored sort of way, with his hands on his hips.

'You start here,' said Kenny. 'The Jenkinses' house. He's a fussy one, that Mr Jenkins, I'll warn you. If the paper gets wet, or crumpled or even the tiniest bit torn, he chucks it out and goes round to old Bingham swearing blue murder. Then of course we get hell. Lots get thrown off the paper round first go, because of him. So watch it!'

'You do it, Marvi!' begged Kathleen, unwilling to take responsibility for the first.

Marvinder extricated the *Daily Mail* and tried rolling it like a rolling pin,

'No, no, no! Not like that. You'll never get it through the letterbox,' cried Ken. 'Like this,' and taking the newspaper, he lightly folded it over, and over again. 'Now it'll go through the letterbox, but the folds will come out when they open it up. The next house has a newspaper, a magazine and a comic. Best thing is to fold the comic into the magazine.' He showed them, taking the *Beano* and folding it into *Titbits*. 'Push that right through first. Then do the *Mirror*, but watch out! Don't put your fingers too far through. They have a dog. Vicious, he is! Loves fingers.'

By the time they had done over twenty or so houses, they had the hang of it. They were five minutes late. Kenny said, 'You'd better get back sharpish if you want the job.'

Kath broke into a run. 'Come on, Marvi!' she begged. 'Let's hurry. We don't want to lose our chance!'

Reluctantly, Marvinder quickened her pace, but still hung back.

'Marvi!' pleaded Kath, puzzled. 'You can move quicker than that. Come on!' She dragged her along by the arm.

They stood before him panting, and Kathy's face was all alarm as Mr Bingham looked at his watch and frowned.

'You're late,' he rasped.

'Sorry, mister. We didn't know. We don't have the time on us, Marvinder and me. We did it all as best we could. Kenny showed us. Give us a chance, mister. We'll be quicker tomorrow. Promise.'

'Well . . . if I get no complaints, you'll stay on. Be here tomorrow, six o'clock sharp.'

'Thanks, mister,' exclaimed Kathleen, full of gratitude. 'We'll be here tomorrow morning, six o'clock sharp! Byee!' And she pulled Marvinder out of the shop, in case he changed his mind.

'We did it! We got a job. Think of the money! Isn't it good?' She jumped up and down gleefully.

Marvinder nodded dumbly. She didn't know what to say. She didn't know how to say the words which clamoured to come out. So she said nothing.

'That's why it's best to get married soon,' pronounced Jhoti. 'The men leave you alone. They wouldn't dare lay a finger on you if you had a husband.'

Marvi was dreaming again. She was riding a horse just as they do in the cowboy films. Galloping, galloping. The horse's hooves thudded into the earth.

Jaspal and his friends often played Cowboys and Indians. They always tried to make Jaspal be an Indian, which made him mad. It was the guns he liked, not bows and arrows. It was guns he was always carving out of bits of wood. The only thing which would have made him give up his turban was to wear a cowboy hat. Some of his friends begged him to loosen his hair and plait it like Indians did, and stick feathers in a headband, but he flatly refused. He was going to be Roy Rogers or the Lone Ranger, turban and all.

Marvinder sometimes joined in, and she didn't mind being an Indian, so long as she could pretend she had a horse.

They played all round the streets and the bomb-sites, racing across other people's gardens, hopping over walls and peering through fences.

'Bang, you're dead!' they shouted.

'Gottcha! Right through the heart!'

'Aaaaah! I'm dying . . . I'm dying . . .'

'I'm dying . . .' a voice whimpered somewhere in the night.

Marvinder half awoke. 'Kathy, did you hear that?' she mumbled.

There was no answer. 'Kathy?' Marvinder stretched out a hand to touch Kathy, but she wasn't there.

The whimpering continued. 'Oh, Jesus Mary . . . I'm dying . . . oh, merciful heaven . . . save me . . .'

Marvinder was filled with terror. 'Kathy?' she whispered. 'Kathy, where are you?'

It was pitch dark. It was as cold as the bottom of a lake. She felt her way to the curtains and drew them back as silently as she could. A pale glimmer just helped her to see the empty bed. She shuffled warily across the the room, carefully avoiding the foldout armchair in which Beryl was sleeping. The door into the hall was open. Now the sobbing was clearer.

'Kathy!'

'Marvi! Marvi, I'm dying,' came a stricken whisper.

Marvinder fumbled for the matches on top of the gas meter. She struck a match. The flame flared brilliantly. The shadows rose gigantic, before diminishing as the flame died down.

100

Kathy was crouched on the stairs in just her nightdress. She was hunched over her knees which she clasped to her chest.

Marvi sprang up to her with alarm. 'Oh, Kathy, what's wrong? Come to bed. You'll catch your death of cold.'

Kathy gazed up at her with terrified eyes. 'Marvi, I'm bleeding to death. Oh, God! I don't know what's happening. I'm covered in blood. I'm going to die, I know it!' The match went out.

Marvinder struck another. Horrified, she saw the dark red stains of blood which streaked Kathy's nightdress.

'Mum! Mum!' She staggered back down the stairs and rushed into the sitting room where the O'Gradys slept on a Put-U-Up sofa bed. 'Mum! Mum! Kathy's bleeding to death!' she cried, stumbling over a chair in the darkness and sprawling across the sleeping couple.

'Jeezuz . . .' Mr O'Grady swore and sat up, murderous with fury at being awoken. 'Who the hell . . .'

'It's only Marvi, Gerry!' Mrs O'Grady quickly pushed him back down into the pillows and patted a blanket over him. 'She's probably having one of her nightmares.' With an exhausted sigh, she heaved her huge body from the sofa. 'What the devil's going on, Marvi?' she demanded in a no-nonsense whisper.

'Kathy says she's dying. She's bleeding to death. Oh, Mum, come quick. She's covered in blood, I tell you.'

'Oh, Mary, Mother of God!' Mrs O'Grady exclaimed. 'What a time to pick. Typical of Kathleen. She chose three in the morning to be born, and now she chooses three in the morning to start the curse.' Grabbing a torch, she lurched out into the hall followed by an alarmed and puzzled Marvinder.

'Has she been cursed, Mum? Will she die?'

Everyone was awake now. Patrick, Michael and Jaspal peered out of their room bleary-eyed. 'What's going on?' they demanded.

'Get back to bed, boys. It's nothing. Just Kathy. She's got tummy ache. Something she ate, I expect. Nothing serious.'

The boys withdrew with relief.

'I'm dying, aren't I, Mum?' wept Kathy.

'No, my love. You're not dying. You've started your monthlies, that's all. You've just become a woman. It'll be Marvinder next. Come on, my duck, let's see to you,' Mum said gently, and led her daughter off to the bathroom.

Mrs O'Grady woke them as usual for the paper round at half-past five the next morning. Kathy didn't seem to mind. On the contrary, Marvinder seemed to detect a sudden change. The panic and bewilderment of the night was wiped away. All in the space of a few hours, Kathy seemed to have developed a superior air, as if somehow, she had suddenly gone one up on Marvinder.

It was a while before Marvinder caught up.

ELEVEN

Voices

Edith lay in her bed; so white the sheets, so pink and flowery her soft eiderdown. She gleamed in the darkness, her golden hair sprayed across the white embroidered pillowcase. Her eyes glimmered like misty stars – awake, but distant. Her body lay still, as if asleep, but her spirit floated far, far away; it floated out, clinging like cobwebs onto the sounds of the violin and piano which she could hear, drifting up from the drawing-room downstairs. Her mother and father were making music together, just as they had always done every day of her life. Just the two of them, united, oblivious to anything else except their love of music and their love for each other. As always, whatever the problems of the day or the anguish of their sorrows, they found comfort in their music and, as always, Edith felt abandoned and excluded.

From her bedroom window, she could see the river. She didn't need to get out of bed to know it was there. It flowed through her brain like a never-ending reminder of the partnership between life and death. If only her mother hadn't broken into their game, she might have learned from Jaspal what it was like to be dead. She might have learned the secret of why Ralph and Grace, though dead, lived on in their parents' hearts just as vividly as if they were alive.

'Somehow,' she resolved to herself, 'I must get hold of Jaspal. We were nearly there. I nearly knew the answer. Jaspal will help me, I know he will.'

But how she would contact Jaspal, she wasn't sure. After the upset of their visit, Harold Chadwick had said it was a mistake ever to have invited Jaspal and Marvinder to the house. It had turned up too many painful memories and upset her mother. Edith lay for a long time, her eyes open, staring into the darkness. She would think of a way.

From her bed which she shared with Kathleen, Marvinder, too, listened. She could hear the faint thin sound of Dr Silbermann playing his violin. Was anything more lonely than the single note, penetrating through the pitiless night, as if seeking its companion, its hope and comfort? It drew Marvinder from her bed, and took her to the top of the back stairs which led down to the basement. She wanted to get out her violin too – the one Dr Silbermann had given her last Christmas. To play music was sometimes the only thing in the world she wanted to do. The violin was like another limb; it was part of her body and soul. Its sound was an inner voice, which could speak and feel things that her own voice couldn't do.

Silently, she opened the door to the back stairs and began to descend, just to be closer. Halfway down, she halted and sat, her arms clasped round herself, to contain her shivering.

'Marvi, my darling, my daughter, my dearest!'

Her mother's voice seemed to be singing inside her head.

'Come to me, sweetheart, don't leave me alone.
For though I am lost, I am looking and longing,
And yearn for the day when you will come home.'

Marvinder rocked herself slowly. 'But, Ma! Are you still alive?' she cried out loud.

'Marvi?' ·

A voice hissed through the darkness behind her, and then a torch flashed and trapped her in its pool of light.

'Good grief, Marvi! What in God's name are you doing sitting down here?'

It was Patrick. 'I thought I heard a voice. Were you talking to someone?' He came down the stairs flashing his torch all around like a searchlight. He was in his stripy pyjamas and bare-footed. She noted how white and bony his feet were, and smiled.

He sat on the step behind her, his knees prodding into her back. 'What are you doing?' he repeated in a sharp whisper.

'Sssh! Just listening to Dr Silbermann,' retorted Marvinder defensively. 'It's nothing to do with you anyway.'

'Yes, it is so. I thought I heard you talking. It could be some burglar who's broken in and was

105

about to kidnap you. Then would you say it's nothing to do with me?'

Marvi giggled. 'Don't be so silly!'

'Me silly? You're the one who's silly. You're the silliest person I ever knew in my life!' His voice rose and broke out of its whisper into laughter.

'Sssh! Everyone'll hear you!' pleaded Marvinder, prodding him with her elbow.

'Well, what could be sillier than sitting on the back stairs in the middle of the night, in the freezing cold, listening to some old geezer playing the violin?' demanded Patrick, nudging her gleefully again with his knees.

Marvinder shifted herself further down the stairs. 'What would you know about Truth and Beauty?' she hissed defiantly.

'Truth and Beauty!' Patrick gave a light whistle. 'My God, he has got at you.' Patrick was silent for a moment, then he said, 'When are you playing in this festival?'

'Not till next month.'

'Can I come and hear you?'

'Don't you dare, Patrick O'Grady. I'll never forgive you if you do.'

'By why, Marvi? Why not? Give me one good reason?'

'Since when did you like the sound of caterwauling, as you call it?' Marvinder challenged him. 'Why should I want to perform in front of someone who thinks I'm only fit to play in the graveyard, along with the cats?'

'Oh, Marvi! I didn't mean it, honest. I was only

teasing. Truthfully, I swear before the sweet Virgin Mary, I want to come and see you play. After all, I might learn about Truth and Beauty if I do. You couldn't deny me that, now, could you?' Somehow his voice, though still teasing, was gentle and friendly.

Marvinder turned and looked at him. She couldn't quite see his face as it was masked behind the beam of the torch. 'Do you mean it?'

'Sure, I mean it. I'd better learn something before I go away.'

'Are you going away?' Marvinder felt an inexplicable quiver of alarm.

'I'll be eighteen next month, and then I do my National Service.'

'What's that?'

'It's the call-up. All boys have to do it, once they're eighteen. Go into the Army or the Navy or the Air Force – you can choose. I'd 'ave gone into the Air Force if I'd had my way, but Mam created such a fuss, I had to give in. I think she'd have laid down on the runway to stop me if I had. She thinks all aeroplanes are dangerous. So, I think I'll choose the Navy. I've always wanted to go to sea. You get to see the world. Perhaps I'll get a ship going to India? What do you think of that? Is it good on ships, Marvi? You came here on a ship, didn't you? The only ship I've been on is a rotten little coffin ship to Ireland. I was sick as a dog all the way over. Marvi?' Patrick realised that Marvinder had not said a word while he had rattled on.

'Patrick! Could I join up? Get a boat and go to

India?' Marvinder leapt to her feet, excitedly. 'Then I could give up the paper round.'

'Sorry, pet!' Patrick patted her comfortingly. 'Girls don't get called up like boys. You could join up later on your own, I suppose, but not for ages. You're only thirteen, aren't you?'

'Nearly fourteen,' Marvinder corrected him.

'Fourteen, then. Still too young. You'll just have to wait. Anyway, what's going to happen? Why go back? Your mother? Me mam says she's more than likely dead. We're your family now, aren't we? I mean what about Maeve and Beryl? Your dad is Beryl's dad too. He can't just leave her. Besides, if you go back, you'll have to marry, won't you? Mammy says you'd have to marry a man your dad chose for you. Could you do that, Marvinder? Marry a man you didn't know and didn't love? It would be a mortal sin – and you only fourteen and all that?'

Marvinder sank back down on to the stairs and buried her head in her arms. They spoke no more to each other, but listened to the pure, singing sound of Dr Silbermann's violin. After a while, when the music stopped, Patrick tugged Marvinder's arm, and guided her back upstairs.

'Goodnight, Patrick.'

'Goodnight, Marvi.' Then before she went into the back room, he whispered, 'Will you let me come then? See you play at the festival?'

'Only if I win. Then you can come to the concert – if that's what you want.'

Patrick waited, shining his torch towards the bed.

Kathleen stirred and rolled over, as Marvinder eased herself in beside her.

Patrick turned the beam of light away and she was plunged into darkness. She wanted to call out, 'Patrick! Don't go.' But he had gone.

Marvinder lay awake long into the night. Her thoughts and feelings tumbled round her brain. They filtered into her blood and were carried by her veins and arteries, tingling, all round her body. 'Patrick.' She whispered his name as if hearing it for the first time.

A girl in a white panama hat was seen around the neighbourhood one day.

Mr O'Grady saw the back of her while selling newspapers on the corner. 'That girl's not from round here,' he thought, noting the smart navy blue and red school uniform. 'We don't get girls wearing panama hats in these parts.' He never saw her face.

The postman saw her as he went about the streets on his bicycle, stopping off at the red pillar boxes to make the third collection of the day. She didn't look lost, yet she didn't look as if she knew what she was doing either. He looked at her curiously. She caught his eye, but rejected his sympathetic glance disdainfully, and turned briskly away.

She popped into Bingham's and bought a stick of liquorice. Mr Bingham tried to engage her in conversation, leaning over the counter in a deliberately friendly manner.

'Haven't seen you in my shop before, my dear

young lady,' he bantered coyly. 'Do you live round here?'

She pushed a penny over the counter without looking at him. 'No. Just visiting,' she said coolly, and left with her liquorice.

Around four o'clock, she was seen hanging round the gates of Christchurch School. Clusters of children jostled by, and a few threw sneery remarks at her. 'Look at her! Proper little snob she must be. Looking for Buckingham Palace, are we? You've come to the wrong place, madam. The King doesn't live round 'ere.'

The girl, as if suddenly realising how conspicuous she was, pulled off her panama hat and folded it under her arm. She walked away from the gates to the end of the railings, then turned and strolled back, trying to appear casual. At the same time, she craned her neck above the hordes of children pouring through the gates. She was looking for someone.

Then she saw him. She knew she couldn't really miss him – even among a hundred children. For sure, he would be the only one with a brown face and wearing a turban. She saw the turban bobbing closer and closer. He seemed to be among a group of boys, some who were his friends – indeed his followers – for he seemed to strut like a leader; but others were enemies – who taunted and jeered and tried to trip him up.

He reached the school gates. 'Jaspal!' He heard his name and turned.

'Edith! What the dickens are you doing here?'

They struggled through the crowds towards each other. Suddenly a big boy broke in between them and flung himself on to Jaspal's back. It was his bitter enemy, Johnnie Cudlip. 'Yeah, yeah, yeah! Ride 'em, cowboy!' he shouted, kicking his heels into Jaspal's sides.

'Yeah, yeah, yeah! Get 'im, Johnnie!' bawled his mates.

'Cloth-head! Blackface! He's nothing but a brainless coolie! Has to wear a bandage to stop his brains from falling out!'

Jaspal staggered and nearly lost his balance. His best friend Billy rushed to his support, but others jumped on him, and soon a fight had started – punching and kicking and strangling and shaking.

The boys tussled and yelled, while supporters on both sides urged them on. Jaspal was spinning round and round, trying to free himself. But Johnnie Cudlip wouldn't let go. He clung like a limpet, forcing his hands over Jaspal's eyes and blinding him.

Edith stared in horror at the scene then, with a cry of rage, she rushed right into the middle of it all, shoving her way through and screaming at the top of her voice. 'Stop it! Stop it, you hooligans. Leave him alone!' She grabbed the boy who clung to Jaspal's back, and hauled him to the ground. 'Leave him alone, you great big bully,' she yelled, and lifted her foot as though she would stamp on him.

The boy rolled into a ball, covering his head protectively. The other children fell away, taken aback by Edith's ferocity. She glared at them all, then picked up her panama hat which had rolled into the gutter and, defiantly, replaced it on her head.

Jaspal crouched on his knees in a daze, trying to retrieve his turban which had got pulled off in the fray. Edith ran over to him and helped him to gather it in and hastily rewind it round his head. Then she said quietly, 'Come on! Let's go,' and as the two set off down the road, the other children stepped aside, muttering and nudging, unable to understand how two such aliens could know each other.

'Are you all right?' asked Edith, anxiously.

'Yeah! I'm fine,' Jaspal grunted. 'It's that Johnnie Cudlip. I'll kill him one of these days. Thanks for your help.' He said it sulkily, though shamefaced. How would he live down being rescued by a girl? 'You shouldn't have interfered. I could have looked after myself. I'm always having fights. What are you doing round here, anyway?'

'I need to talk to you. I want to try again.'

'What do you mean, try again?' frowned Jaspal.

'What we did when you came over last Saturday. When you told me about how the twins drowned and what it felt like to die. You nearly told me, but then Mummy came in before you finished, and spoilt it all.'

People were staring at them in the street. Edith suddenly felt awkward.

'Where can we go to talk?' she muttered, as a passing child jeered, 'Who's your lady friend, Jaspal?'

'We could go on the common,' suggested Jaspal, but he too felt awkward being seen with Edith.

'I know. We'll go on the underground. That's how I came. I got a return ticket back to Richmond. You can get a thruppenny return ticket and not leave the underground. At least we'll be able to talk without seeing people who know you.'

'I haven't got thruppence,' grunted Jaspal. He wished she hadn't come. He wasn't sure he wanted to play that game again. It had revived too many painful memories.

'I have,' said Edith taking out three pennies from her school purse. 'Come on!' And she assertively herded him towards the underground sign they could see in the distance.

It was a strange journey, taking the Northern Line to King's Cross, plunging into the bowels of the earth, watching reflections of themselves, like ghosts, mirroring their huddled conversations as they talked and talked; and people swept in and out like debris on the tide. And sometimes Edith broke into Punjabi, and Jaspal laughed to hear her, and she laughed too. People stared at them, but they were strangers, and neither Edith nor Jaspal cared; and by the time they had changed on to the Circle Line and were heading first westwards then southwards down to Gloucester Road, they were deep in a discussion about Deri, their village in India, and the fun they had had when they all lived there: that is, until the twins were born, and Edith was sent far away to school in Simla; then there were the holidays when she came home, hating Ralph and Grace, because they hardly left her any room to be with her parents – and their drowning seemed like a devil's answer to her prayer.

'I was born in India – so I'm as Indian as you,' she exclaimed passionately. 'One day, I shall go back. I know I will. You too, yes?'

Jaspal shrugged. 'Yes. I want to go home. Perhaps Ma is alive . . .' his voice trailed away as terrible images flooded back into his mind. 'You didn't see the troubles,' he whispered harshly. 'You didn't see how they killed everyone. Everyone . . . my friends, my aunts and uncles – even children and babies. Perhaps my mother.' He paused while he violently dashed his eyes against his sleeve. 'They burned our houses and destroyed our temple. They tried to wipe us from the face of the earth as if we were ants. When I go back, I'll go back to take revenge. I swear I'll do to them what they did to me.' Jaspal's fists were clenched in his lap, so that his knuckles gleamed white.

Edith leaned back, shocked by his rage. She watched the reflection of his face in the window. It had become hard and cruel.

After a while, she said, 'I must find out . . . I need to know . . . about the twins.' She turned and looked at him. 'You understand what I mean, don't you?'

'I understand revenge,' Jaspal answered slow and fierce. 'Is that what you want? Perhaps you should kill me. I took Ralph and Grace to the lake. I suggested going out in the boat. If it's revenge you want, then kill me.' He was nearly shouting now. He jumped up and pulled apart his shirt, exposing his throat.

The heads of other passengers turned in curiosity at this outbreak, and Edith pulled him down, trying to shush him up. 'No, no, no! I don't want revenge. It wasn't your fault, but mine. I was meant to be looking after them, and you were as young as they were – too young to be responsible. I made Marvinder run away from them with me. I was the one who wanted them dead – don't you see? Now I want to say sorry. If I can only say sorry . . . That's why I need you to help me contact them. I've heard that the dead can be contacted. We nearly did it, didn't we? You felt it too. Admit it. Let's try. Just one more time, Jaspal. Promise me you'll help me.'

Jaspal flopped down in his seat again with his head lowered. 'How? Will you dress up again? Play the same game?' he sneered.

'It's not a game. You know it's not. It's a way – the only way I know of. But don't tell anyone – not even Marvinder. She didn't want to do it. She didn't believe in it . . . but you did. I know you did. I don't need anyone else – just you. Come to Richmond. We have a boat. Let's take it out on the river. We'll go in the night. I know their spirits live on in the water. Sometimes I look out of my window, and I almost think I can see them floating by. Do you realise – all the waters in the world join up. I know they do – and the twins are here, in England . . . in the waters of the river, floating past our house. If I could only talk to them . . . tell them . . .'

'Tell them what?' Jasper shuddered.

'Tell them I'm sorry. Sorry they're dead. I didn't really want them dead. I thought I did, till they were gone, and now, if I could bring them back . . . If I could die and make them live, I would gladly kill myself.'

'Edith!'

'You talk of revenge,' she murmured bitterly. 'Perhaps I should take revenge on myself.'

They reached Gloucester Road and changed again, this time waiting for a District Line train to take Edith back to Richmond. They were silent now; exhausted by their exchanges. They stared at the rails.

'Come on Saturday night!' said Edith quickly as they heard the rumble of an approaching train. 'My parents are going to a concert. They'll be out all evening. If you came at about nine o'clock, the babysitter, Mrs Bourne, usually dozes off by then. It would be dark, and we can take the boat out on the river and . . . you'll help me, won't you, to make contact with the twins? They were your friends. Promise me, Jaspal.' She clasped his arm in a vice and wouldn't let go. The train came in; the doors opened. She stepped inside, but still gripped his arm as he stood on the platform. 'Promise me. Say you'll come to my house on Saturday night. I'll never ask anything of you ever again, if you do this one thing. I only want to tell the twins I'm sorry. Say you'll come!'

Her cheeks burned red as if she were feverish.

116

'Say it!' The doors were closing, but she didn't let go.

'All right!' shouted Jaspal, and snatched his arm away.

He saw her wild face, still staring intently at him as the train carried her away, and still saw it long after the train had disappeared. Then wearily he turned and crossed over to the other platform to start his long journey home.

TWELVE

Savage Soul

The teacher had thought he was carrying home a simple, unfortunate boy – another victim of the troubles. His old aunt, a dour, unsmiling, dry woman who lived with him, cooked and attended to him with utter devotion, seemed quite pleased to be given a child to care for. She had hurried forward frowning with alarm, when he arrived back after his usual evening walk, carrying this small, thin, dangling creature. But when he laid it on the bed and she saw how young it was – barely out of its infancy – yet its body as hard and shrivelled as an old man's, all her maternal feelings rushed into her heart and, for the first time in ages, her face softened.

'Poor little thing! How did he get a wound like that?' she cried, seeing the gash on its head. 'Look at it – all covered in sores and scratches; and its belly hard and swollen with malnutrition.' She rushed off to get a bucket of water.

As she washed it down gently, cleaning away the blood from its face, she marvelled at the long, curling, uncut nails on its fingers and toes, and its hair like a tangled thorn bush. 'Why, it hardly looks human.'

It was the middle of the night when the child regained consciousness. The teacher and his aunt woke to hear a terrible spitting and squealing; and banging and crashing. They rushed from their beds; it was as though the devil had been let loose inside their home. At first they didn't realise it was the child. A creature – more like a wildcat – flung itself around the room, clawing and hissing and leaping at the barred window. As they came in through the door, the child flung itself towards the opening, but the teacher slammed the door shut behind him. The child backed into a corner, and gathered itself into a feline crouch, ready to spring. It stared at him with glowering eyes and howled and howled, so piteously, so loudly and unremittingly, that the teacher finally spread out his hands in surrender and murmured, 'All right, little Jungli. Who am I to keep you prisoner if you want to go?' and turning his back, he left the room, leaving the door wide open. Only the faintest sound, and something brushing passed his legs, made him realise that the child had fled into the night.

For a long time, the teacher sat on the verandah shocked and despairing. He couldn't make sense of the world. There was chaos in everything. It was as though the child was India gone wild; just like the men who had torn the country limb from limb; just like the fanatic who had shot the Mahatma; like the gardens of the palace – once so ordered and cared for – now run wild with savage seed. They had all strayed across the boundary between human and beast. Could they ever be tamed again?

'I'll leave a bowl of milk and honey for him,' said Aunt gently. 'Even the wildest animal can be defeated by hunger.'

The teacher nodded dumbly, and went on staring into the void.

By morning, the milk had gone. The teacher gazed at the empty dish and then at his old aunt, who clasped her hands with quiet triumph. 'Didn't I say?' she whispered.

Of course, they couldn't be certain that it was the wild child who had drunk it and, for many days, they scoured the district for some sight of him. But each evening, the old aunt left a bowl of milk at the bottom of the verandah steps, and each morning it was gone.

'We'll put the milk out at dawn, before I say my prayers,' said the teacher. 'Perhaps we'll then see who comes to drink the milk.' So nothing was left out that night and, in the first grey glimmer of early morning, before the schoolteacher had washed, said his prayers and dressed, he left a shallow metal dish full of milk and honey out on the little verandah, and waited.

There was a strange hush. Even the crows seemed to hold back their dawn clamour – watching the grey, silent fields which lay beyond the compound. The teacher strained his eyes into the deep shadows within the mango and guava groves; no light had yet penetrated the deep ditches alongside the road, and a wild scrubland straggled and faded to black within the abyss of the jungle.

His appearance was sudden. So sudden that it

was as if the teacher had simply blinked, and in that moment, the child was there, his nose down in the milk, lapping like a puppy.

The teacher smiled.

Each morning at dawn, the teacher put out the milk and honey. Each morning he spied the wild child approaching the dish as warily as a fox and lapping up the contents, speedily, ravenously, sucking up every drop, before darting away. Once, another creature had got to the dish first. A snake was lapping, its forked tongue shooting out into the sweet, white liquid.

Now what? thought the teacher, alarmed. He braced himself, ready to intervene. But the child just sat patiently at a distance, waiting until the snake had had its fill and glided away, then he lolloped up happily, and finished off the rest.

'Aunt, I'll try leaving the milk at the top of the steps this time,' said the teacher, one day. 'See if I can persuade him to come into the bungalow.' So next time he left the bowl at the top of the verandah steps and then after a few days, moved the bowl further and further along the verandah. One morning, the teacher came out and stood there, just watching the boy. Aware of his presence, the boy looked up, stared and then carried on drinking. The teacher beckoned to his aunt. With silent joy, they watched the child finish the milk then, casually licking its lips in a satisfied way, amble off into the trees beyond the compound.

Day by day it became more trustful; it stayed longer and sometimes even took to curling up in the shade of the verandah to escape the heat of the day. The teacher began to devise more ploys to attract the child and get it to stay, for he was determined to tame it.

The wild child scrabbled about on all fours, as though it had never learned to walk on two feet. It didn't use its fingers to eat, but lapped water and took food directly into his mouth like an animal. The teacher put out a table, and placed the bowl on the table, hoping to force the child to stand on two legs to reach the food. The first time, the boy leapt right onto the table itself, knocking over the flimsy structure and sending his milk flying all over the place. He screamed with rage, and dashed his face at the empty dish, licking up what remnants he could from the stone verandah. The teacher picked up the table, refilled the bowl and put it back in the same place. The same thing happened again and again; the boy fled into the undergrowth, howling with hunger and frustration. But the teacher persevered and at last, one day, Jungli gripped the sides of the table with his hands and stood up on his two legs. He tried to reach the bowl, lunging his head forward with protruding lips and tongue outstretched. But it was no use. Then, at last, he reached out a hand. His gnarled, clawlike fingers touched the metal; he gripped; pulled it closer – and tipped it, overflowing the contents into his mouth. The teacher was victorious.

Aunt wanted to clothe the boy. For her, that was the next important step. 'He won't look human till he is clothed,' she cried. She made him a loose kurta

– a thin, long, cotton tunic and begged her nephew to put it on the child. The teacher tried every way; first by coaxing him, then by leaving it around for the boy to play with and perhaps to pull on for himself. Finally he tried using the element of surprise; one day, when the boy had just finished eating, he slipped the shirt onto his back.

Aunt rushed out with alarm, thinking something terrible was happening. But what she saw was a life and death struggle between a boy and a shirt. He flayed around, his arms pounding through the material, his nails and teeth ripping at the cloth. When the teacher tried to intervene he bit the teacher's hand and made him howl with pain. At last, Jungli tore off the offending garment and, leaving it shredded in the dust, scampered off on all fours, shrieking, as if for all the world he had put on a shirt made of stinging nettles.

'Oh, look at it!' cried the aunt in dismay. 'And to think this morning, that was a newly stitched kurta. Now it's only fit for use as a rag to polish my pots.'

Aunt also made up a soft comfortable bed hoping that the boy might be tempted to sleep in it. They knew the boy was nocturnal, but they had still not discovered where it finally laid its body down to rest – night or day. But for the boy, the bed was only a place to play. They would hear him at night, grunting and sniffing as he burrowed under the blanket or shook the edge of the sheet in his teeth like a puppy. Then there was silence, and they knew he had gone.

'He must sleep somewhere,' murmured the aunt, and took to wandering around the area, trying to imagine where a wild creature would make its bed. At last, one afternoon, she discovered him; quite close by, sleeping high up in a tree, his body looped between the fork of two branches.

One day, the child didn't appear. Just when the teacher and his aunt thought that the child had got used to coming to them each day, suddenly, he didn't come. They were alarmed, and searched through the undergrowth and all round the district. Three, four and five days went by, and still the milk, which they continued to put out, was untouched.

Many nights later, the teacher awoke. He heard something. Had the child returned? Then he thought he heard the snort of a creature, and the scraping of hooves. He ran out into the darkness and stood in the middle of the yard, an oil lantern swinging from his hand. He could smell the scent of jasmine and marigolds and the Star of Bethlehem – which only flowered at night – mingling with the musky odour of animal. He noticed the earth had been scuffed up and, lying freshly scattered in the dust, were flower petals. He remembered the horse. The mysterious white horse which had haunted the district. Had it come to his door?

Unable to sleep for the rest of the night, he felt a sudden compulsion to write a letter. It was to the Secretary of the Church Missionary Society in London.

Most Honoured Sir,

I hope you will forgive my presumption in writing to your most gracious person. I am nothing but a simple schoolmaster from the village of Deri in the Punjab, India. I am eternally grateful to have benefited from being educated by your inestimable organisation. I attended the mission school when it was run by the most revered and respected Mr Harold Chadwick. With his help and encouragement, I proceeded on to Amritsar University from where I graduated with a B.A. and then returned to my village to become a teacher.

As you no doubt will be aware, we have been in the throes of terrible troubles as a result of the partition of India. My school was burnt down, as were most of the properties in the district. Many of my pupils and their families were killed or forced to flee.

I have been cycling to the next village, where there is still a school building, and have been endeavouring to teach as best I can with hardly any help and no proper salary.

However, my greatest desire is to restore the school here in my own village; the one which was once run by our respected and dearly beloved Mr Chadwick. I wish to educate the homeless, stateless and fatherless children who, at present, roam the district like animals. But the task is great and I have no help on which I can count. I have no books, no writing materials and no money. That is why I take this unpardonable liberty of writing to you.

I hope that you still remember this school, which you founded and built, and could discover in your heart the desire to take an interest once more and help me to restore it. Our country has run wild. Without education we are savages. Help us to help ourselves.

I remain, dear sir,
Your most respected, humble and obedient servant,
Bahadhur Manmohan Singh

He wrote and rewrote his letter many times, polishing it up and checking his ant-eaten English dictionary for correct spellings. Then, with a sigh of satisfaction, he sealed it in a thin white envelope. Early next morning, he cycled seven miles down the road to the shack which acted as post office, huddled into the shady skirts of a tall, sweeping grey cotton tree. The sleepy *babuji* who sat cross-legged on a cracked wooden counter dropped the letter on to a pair of scales, adding the smallest of his weights to the other side. 'Uh huh! England, eh!' he muttered, fishing for information with which he could gossip over for the rest of the day.

'Yes, England!' murmured the teacher, but said no more.

'Bublu? What's wrong?' asked Sparrow, winding his thin arms around his protector's neck. 'Are you sad?' Every nuance of Bublu's moods affected Sparrow; when Bublu was cheerful he whistled and sang at the top of his voice and Sparrow did too; when Bublu was brave, Sparrow walked in his shadow trying to absorb his bravery, emulating his cocky strut and cool demeanour. But to see the older boy looking withdrawn and depressed terrified him.

'Are you worried about One Eye? You don't have to take any notice of him. I've heard the others talking. They all think he's stupid. No one wants him for a leader. They only want you.'

'I no longer care about being the leader,' murmured Bublu. 'If One Eye wants to take over, let him. I don't even want to stay here any more.'

When he heard that, Sparrow became panic-stricken. 'Are you going? You will take me with you, won't you? You wouldn't leave me, would you, Bublu? Please don't leave me.' He fell weeping at Bublu's feet, clutching his ankles as if to root him to the ground. Ever since Sparrow had lost his whole family, Bublu had become mother, father, sister and brother to him.

'Arreh!' Bublu gently released himself from the young boy's grasp and heaved him up onto his hip. 'Don't worry. I'll always look after you.'

'What do you want to do? Where do you want to go?' asked Sparrow, swallowing deep breaths of relief.

'First, I want to catch that horse. It spooked me before. I was an idiot. I let it go, when I could have hopped on its back easy as jumping a gate. Just because of that Jungli I went to pieces. But a horse is just a horse, and I'm going to find it and make it mine.'

'Then what will you do?' gasped Sparrow, full of awe.

'I'll ride it, of course. I'll climb on its back and dig my heels into its sides and we'll gallop away – far away.'

'Where, Bublu, where?' cried Sparrow.

'Wherever!' answered Bublu nonchalantly. 'Who cares where? Wherever the horse wants to go.'

'And you'll take me with you?' whispered Sparrow, full of dread again.

'Yes, *bhai*! It's a big horse. It's like a war-horse – a warrior's horse. There's room for you to ride behind.'

'What if it's Jungli's horse?' The question hung ominously in the air.

'How could it be?' retorted Bublu, loud enough to stifle his own doubts.

But Bublu knew Sparrow was right, wherever the horse had been seen so, too, had Jungli. 'From now on, we both keep our eyes and ears open, and we don't tell a soul, do you understand?' He thought of his encounter with his teacher. He had half recognised him. It put Bublu even more on his guard. 'If the authorities get wind of us, we'll all be taken away to orphanages – split up – and you wouldn't want that, would you?'

Sparrow shuddered at the thought.

At sunset, Bublu had slipped away as usual, and climbed to the uppermost terrace of the palace to say his evening prayers in secret, unobserved – or so he thought.

But One Eye knew. One Eye wanted power and revenge. He knew he couldn't get it by a physical fight with Bublu. Bublu wasn't a leader just because he was very strong. Bublu was a leader because the others respected him and trusted his judgement. One Eye knew he must destroy that confidence. He must bring Bublu into disrepute. He would get power by stealth.

So he watched everyone; storing up bits of knowledge which would add to his power and give him a hold over them. He listened to their ravings in the night; the mutterings in their sleep which gave them away. He noted the Hindu and the manner in which he bathed in the lake each morning; he noted the Sikh hair cut, to be sure, and no sign of the knife, comb or steel bangle; but being a Sikh himself, he recognised the signs: the shorts – and the thread around the waist. And as for Bublu, he had noted how the boy would slip away; he had followed him up to the terraces above, and see him prostrate himself in the direction of Mecca. Bublu was a Muslim. Everyone in these parts hated Muslims.

One Eye had harboured this knowledge for a long time, waiting for the moment when it would come in useful. He gloated over his secrets like a miser gloats over gold. Bit by bit, he had become powerful and now was the time to test it.

'Hey, Sparrow!' One Eye sauntered menacingly up to the young boy.

Sparrow shrank away from him. 'What do you want?' he asked.

'I heard there were Muslims in the district, on the rampage. Slitting the throats of Hindus and Sikhs.' He drew a finger across the boy's throat and laughed at his terror. 'You'd better run and hide before they get you too.'

Sparrow looked desperately around for Bublu.

'Looking for Bublu? What makes you think he can help – the stinking pig! You think Bublu would help you? Why, Bublu will probably be the one to kill you. He's just waiting for the right moment, in the still of the night, while you're asleep, he'll get out his knife and – slit – ' he whipped a finger across his throat – 'that'll be it for you.'

'What do you mean?' stammered Sparrow, aghast at such terrible words. 'Bublu's my friend. He's always been my friend. He wouldn't hurt a hair of my head. You're just a liar.'

'That's where you're wrong, you little snivelling worm.' One Eye suddenly grabbed him. He was much, much bigger and Sparrow couldn't struggle. He opened his mouth to scream Bublu's name, but One Eye slammed a hand over his mouth. 'You just shut up! I'll show you your beloved Bublu. Just shut up and I'll take you to him. One peep out of you and I'll break your arms, do you hear?'

Almost collapsing with terror, Sparrow nodded. One Eye marched him up the steep stone steps – up to the first terrace, then the second and finally up to the third – to the very top of the palace.

'I wonder in which direction is Mecca!' hissed

One Eye. He held the boy's head in a vice-like grip and forced it round. 'North, south, east . . . no, west, I believe – over there where the sun is setting.' He marched him round, till they faced the last deep rosy sky, where the sun had just dipped below the rim of the horizon.

'You see! There's your beloved Bublu! He's nothing but a Muslim. Hey, Sparrow, meet a murderer! The killer of your mother and father!' proclaimed One Eye, releasing Sparrow and shoving him forward towards Bublu, who crouched on his knees in prayer, with head bowed towards Mecca.

One Eye was laughing – laughing like a maniac. Bublu got slowly to his feet without turning round. He gazed out over the blood-red lake; and then he saw the horse. There on the shore, shining white against the darkening sky. It seemed to be waiting for him. He turned and grabbed Sparrow. 'Come.' He dragged the limp child to the steps, and began the long descent to the ground, while One Eye yelled with glee, 'He's going to kill you! He's going to kill you!'

The other boys came running and shouting. 'What's happening? Is there another raid?' There was panic and confusion. Bublu burst through them all, thrusting aside grasping hands which tried to hold him when One Eye yelled, 'Bublu is a Muslim! Catch the murderer! He killed my family. He burnt down my house. He spat on my God. Don't let him go. He's going to kill Sparrow.'

Sparrow was moaning as, like some rag doll,

Bublu dragged him tumbling and flopping down the stone steps and out across the wild palace lawns into the deepening shadows.

'The horse has come! The horse has come. It's come for us. It's come to save us!' cried Bublu. They reached the shore. The horse didn't move. Bublu lifted the fainting Sparrow onto his hip and staggered on, more slowly, but steadily with hand outstretched. The horse whinnied gently. Bublu took the loose reins. He slung Sparrow onto its back. 'Hold tight,' he whispered, and dragged the horse over to a fallen tree on the edge of the shore. It stood placidly, while Bublu climbed onto the tree trunk and, grabbing the horse's long mane, hauled himself on to its back.

The other boys were racing towards them, hollering death cries as they fanned out across the shore. Bublu dug his heels into the horse's sides. He felt its warm, quivering body move into action. It moved like a running river: powerful, smooth, confident, whirling round rocks and boulders and over logs and low walls; it galloped on and on towards the dark jungle, its hooves drumming like a beating heart.

'Allah Akbar! God is great!' yelled Bublu ecstatically.

THIRTEEN

Love or Duty?

'Do you remember the story of Rama and Sita?'
Jhoti asked her daughter.

'Oh yes, Ma! It's my favourite story – how Prince
Rama and the beautiful Princess Sita were banished
from the Kingdom of Ayodhya for fourteen years.
How they lived in the jungle and Sita was kidnapped by Ravana, the ten-headed king of the
demons. I spent almost all night telling Kathleen
that story, and scared her to death when I told her
about the demons – especially Ravana with his ten
heads!'

'Did you know, Marvinder, my daughter, that,
when after fourteen long years of searching, Rama
finally found Sita, he rejected her? Can you believe
that? I know I shouldn't say this, but when I first
heard this story as a very young child, I couldn't
understand how Rama could say that he loved Sita,
and then reject and humiliate her in this way; and
he didn't just reject her once, he rejected her twice.
The second time, there was no one to speak for her
as Agni, the god of fire had done; the second time,
Rama just told his brother, Lakshmana, to take her
away, deep into the jungle and leave her to live
with the old hermit, Valmiki.'

'And when you grew up, Ma, did you then understand why Rama rejected Sita?'

'I understood that it was because Rama was a god and not an ordinary man; that he was upholding God's laws. Rama as man would have received back his wife with total joy, no matter what had happened to her, but Rama as a god, could not take her back if she had been ravished by Ravana, for Sita too is a goddess – and there could be no shadow of defilement about her person. Yet the stories tell us that Sita was cruelly hurt by Rama's rejection, and what I couldn't understand, and still don't is, if Rama was a god, why did he not have the power to make his people see that Sita was innocent? By sending her away, he was giving in to the foul thoughts of ordinary humans. Even Sita didn't understand, so how could I?

'I too am in exile, Marvinder, my daughter. I too am waiting to be rescued. But will my husband reject me as Rama did?'

'Oh, Ma!' Marvinder was filled with anguish. How could she know what her father, Govind, would do? How could she know what was right any more?

'If my father rejects you, it won't be because he is a god,' murmured Marvinder. Then wondered if her mother had heard that. 'What I mean is, my father isn't a god, Ma. He is a very weak human being and it will take him longer to weigh up and choose between love and duty – if he can even tell where his duty lies.'

'Yes, that's it . . .' Jhoti's voice sighed and thinned

*away into nothing as she said, 'Love and duty...
we need gods to show us...'*

Saturday night was always a busy night. Mr and
Mrs O'Grady went to the Irish club along the High
Road, while Patrick, Michael and Maeve went
dancing, sometimes at the local dance hall, but at
least once a month at the Hammersmith Palais.

So everyone was in a flurry of getting spruced
up. Mr O'Grady would give himself a really close
shave and, with the tweezers, pluck out a few hairs
from his eyebrows or ears. Then he carefully
brought forth his one and only suit – the one he
was married in – and hung it from the doorway to
let the creases fall out. Mrs O'Grady would unwind
her curlers which she had had in all day and try to
comb her hair into a fashionable bob. Then she too
would put on her one best dress – and, after she
had dabbed the tiniest few drops of lavender water
behind her ears, she felt like the Queen of England.

Patrick and Michael took themselves off to the
public baths, where for sixpence they could get
themselves a thoroughly good, long, steamy, deep
bath with plenty of soap. How they loved lying in
the green water, semi-floating, while the grime of
the week slid out from under their fingernails and
hair and from the pores of their skin. How they
loved singing, and hearing their voices bounce off
the hard, white tiles loud as opera singers, and
being told good-naturedly to 'Shut up!' by others
in cubicles further down. Then they would return
home red as boiled lobsters from having lain too

long in very hot water, and would vie with each other to get in front of the mirror so that they could Brylcreme their hair sleek and shining as film stars.

Upstairs, Maeve refused to be left behind and insisted on going dancing with her brothers. 'Why shouldn't I enjoy myself too?' She and her mother had rowed bitterly over how much Maeve liked to go out.

'You're a married woman, my girl, just you remember that – and a mammy too.'

'Yes, but I'm young – and the world isn't standing still just because Govind's in prison. Anyway, why should I be punished because of what he did?' So there she was upstairs, determinedly painting her nails, powdering her face and and putting bright red lipstick on her tight, angry lips. After all, she thought with self-justification, it's me own brothers I'm going with, not some sailor on shore leave.

Marvinder and Kathleen always felt like proper little Cinderellas; helping Mrs O'Grady take the curlers out of her hair, ironing shirts and polishing shoes for the men, and then, while they all went off to enjoy themselves, being left at home to look after Beryl. How they wished they were old enough to go dancing too.

'Here, give us a going over, Marvi,' cried Patrick, tossing her a clothes brush. 'Make sure I don't have any dandruff on me, won't you. Can't have girls pressing their faces into my shoulder if I'm covered in dandruff!' He winked at her.

Marvi stood on tiptoe to brush his collar and shoulders, and wished more than anything, that she could go dancing with him. She took rather longer than was necessary to brush him down – finally saying, 'There now! Not one speck of dust on you anywhere . . . but . . .'

'But what?' he whirled round anxiously.

'You smell of mothballs, Patrick O'Grady. Will the girls want to dance with you smelling like the inside of a wardrobe?'

'Why, you cheeky monkey!' he laughed, grabbing her plaits and winding them round her neck as if to strangle her.

Then Maeve appeared in the doorway. Michael whistled. 'Hey! Take a look at Rita Hayworth!'

There was Maeve, her deep red hair all swept into a long bob, so that one side fell partly over her face, and the other showed her long, white neck. Her dress was green to match her eyes; it was slinky and tight-fitting and swirled out at the bottom. She had put on stockings – nylons – which she had got from an American soldier the last time she went dancing, and high-heeled shoes which made her legs look long and shapely – just like the film stars. Suddenly, Marvinder felt her insides freeze. Yes, men here liked girls to look like Rita Hayworth and Jane Russell. Kathleen too would look like her sister very soon – and she'd wear dresses pulled in tight at the waist, and have bobbed red hair, fashionably, and paint her fingernails and lips; and she would go dancing and men would want to take her to the pictures – men like Michael . . . or . . . Patrick . . . Marvinder released herself from his hands. Would Patrick ever look at a girl like her?

'Thanks, my precious,' he murmured, going over to the mirror to check himself once more. 'You'd better watch out, girls! Here I come,' he murmured admiringly. Marvinder felt she had become invisible.

Jaspal clattered down the stairs shouting, 'Cheerio!' He usually went out roaming with his mates on Saturday nights and no one bothered to ask him where he was going.

'Make sure you're home by the time we are!' Mrs O'Grady reminded him.

The door slammed without an answer. 'He gets away with everything just because he's a boy,' hissed Kathleen. 'Why is life so unfair?'

So, that Saturday, Mr and Mr O'Grady set off for the Irish club, he on his bike – for, one-legged that he was, that was the best way for him to get around – and she, striding along not so far behind, carrying his crutches. Patrick, Michael and Maeve waited for the bus, trying not to let the wind ruffle their carefully coiffured hair. Kathleen, Marvinder and Beryl watched enviously from the window until the trolleybus came and whisked them all away.

'Wish we could go dancing,' sighed Marvinder.

'Hey, Marvi, do you know any dances? Come here!' Kathleen grabbed Marvinder and forced her arms into a tango position. 'Burrrr . . . uum tum tum tum, boom der di der dum derr . . . rum tum tum tum,' she sang, as she led them across the floor, turned with a jerk and returned while Beryl chortled with glee.

'You have to be very proud – like a Spanish senorita. You should see Patrick do it. He's as good as Fred Astaire. What a mover – especially when he dances with Irene. Brrum tum tum tum ... brrrum der di der dum der rrrum tum tum tum ...'

'Who's Irene?' Marvinder found herself choking over the name.

'A girl he walks out with sometimes. She's very beautiful and she moves like this ...' and Kathleen lifted her chin high in the air and swept Marvinder around the room still singing loudly. 'She looks like Vivien Leigh ... mmm ...'

'Me now, Kathy! Dance with me!' begged Beryl trying to break in.

'I haven't seen her.' Marvinder tried to sound casual as she stopped to extricate Beryl from between their knees.

'Patrick never brings her round here. He always meets her at the Palais or up the West End. I think she's posh, and Patrick doesn't want her to see the kind of neighbourhood he lives in!'

'Are they going to get married?' Marvinder whispered her question, but could hardly bear to hear the answer.

'I dunno. They're not engaged or anything ... but I think Patrick's quite soft on her. He'll know better once he's done his National Service – that's what Mummy says. Cor! I can't wait to see Patrick in his uniform. All the girls will fall for him –

including Irene. Come on, Beryl!' Kathleen lifted her niece up into her arms. 'Let's dance!' and she whirled the child round the room singing, 'All the nice girls love a sailor . . .'

In the downstairs flat immediately below them, Mr Beard took up his walking stick and prodded the ceiling angrily.

Jaspal waited. Why had he come? He felt annoyed with himself for being so easily commanded by Edith. He should have stood up to her – she shouldn't think she could come the memsahib with him. He wondered if she remembered their arrangement. He'd give her half an hour then, if she didn't appear, he'd go home. He hoped she had forgotten. He felt uneasy playing her game with just the two of them. He wished now he had told Marvinder.

He heard someone whistling, and the steady fall of approaching feet. A policeman strolled into view, his eye scanning the houses as he passed. Jaspal dropped to his knees, feeling like a thief. The policeman seemed to pause, just for a second and look a little longer, before carrying on. When he had gone, Jaspal crept out of the bushes and swiftly moved round to the back of the house. He crept up to the back door and peered in through the glass. He could see the distant glimmer of a hall light. How long was he supposed to wait? Would she come to the front or the back? They hadn't made a proper arrangement. That was it. That was the excuse. At least he had come. It wasn't his fault if he didn't know where he was supposed to wait – or for how long.

Jaspal had come to Edith's house by underground. It was barely dark when he got to Richmond. The days were getting longer all the time and there was still the silvery grey light of dusk even though it was nine o'clock. He had made his way to Edith's house. One light was on downstairs, and another on the second floor – in Edith's bedroom. He moved silently, through the gate and up the path. He couldn't knock at the door, so he crossed the front lawn and stood on tiptoe among the hydrangea bushes in the flower bed, to peer in through the bay window. The living-room curtains were not quite drawn to, and he could just see through the gap.

Mrs Bourne, the babysitter, was comfortably ensconced in the large, wing-backed armchair before a quietly glowing fire. Every now and then her fingers went into a flurry of needles and wool as she flew into her knitting which lay gathered on her lap. But then, after a few minutes, her movements slowed down and, like a clockwork doll whose spring had unwound, she came to a stop, the needles poised in her hands. At this point, her chin dropped forward on to her chest and she dozed.

As he watched, Edith suddenly came into the room. She was wearing her dressing-gown. She stood for some moments observing Mrs Bourne – was she asleep? Jaspal could see the question on Edith's face. She moved deliberately round the

141

room, keeping her eyes on the old lady's face. Then, finally satisfied, Edith left the room.

The last of the daylight ebbed away and the house seemed suddenly dark and empty. Jaspal felt a knot of unease tighten in his stomach. He was tempted to run. A great moon hung low, tossed among swiftly-moving clouds as though it too was caught in a swirling river. Sometimes it disappeared from sight completely, and the night became blacker, then it re-emerged like a swimmer fighting to keep afloat. Jaspal began backing down the path.

'Jaspal? Are you there?' A torch light bounced around him from a window above.

He stopped. 'Yes!'

'Stay where you are. I'm coming down.'

There she goes again, handing out orders. Edith never just seemed to say anything normally; she always commanded. He didn't like it. He'd tell her so one day. Another five minutes passed by. It seemed to be an age but, at last, he saw the torchlight bobbing towards him and there she was, wearing a skirt and jumper under her blazer.

'Let's get going,' she hissed. 'We only have about an hour. Come on!' Edith marched ahead and led him across the long back garden which sloped down to the river. The great shining surface suddenly confronted them in the evening light, as the path dropped beneath the overhanging willows. Edith pointed to a small wooden landing-stage where a rowing boat was moored.

At the sight of the boat and oars, Jaspal was suddenly overcome with panic. Memories surged back more vividly than ever. The moon turned into an Indian sun, flashing on the water. He was leading Rani, his water buffalo, down to the water's edge; the twins were riding on her back, laughing with delight. They slid to the ground as the great beast eased herself into the cool lake. Jaspal heard his voice pointing out the boat. 'Let's row across the lake to the island.' Out there in the middle was the old stone gazebo with its ornate cupola which, like an open umbrella, created a dark purple shade, to protect and cool the maharajahs while they fished. How eagerly they scrambled to the boat, pushing it off the shore and heaving themselves in. Jaspal could smell again the old rotting wood and the slosh of stagnant water; he could feel the splintery roughness against his bare feet and then the rocking motion and the silkiness of the water as they dipped their arms over the side.

'Get in.' Edith's whisper was as sharp as the edge of steel.

Jaspal obeyed. The boat tipped as it received his weight, and tipped again, as Edith unlooped the rope and then climbed in. The boat drifted away from the bank. Jaspal picked up the oars and fitted them into the rungs.

'Where are we going?' he asked, looking over his shoulder into the liquid void. Edith faced him, her knees clenched tightly together, her hands too, clasped in front. Her face was white and hard like a porcelain doll. Her eyes stared ahead without blinking. She didn't answer. He dipped the oars into the water, just to guide them on a straighter course, for, already, a current had taken charge of the boat.

When they were some distance from the shore, Edith suddenly turned, swung her legs over the seat and moved to the very stern of the boat. Lying flat on her stomach, she trailed both arms in the water, not caring that her sleeves were instantly drenched.

'Edith, what are you doing?' gasped Jaspal with alarm. He looked up and down the towpath. There was no one about at all. Only on the far side did he dimly perceive a man walking his dog – but in the other direction and soon out of sight.

'Did you know,' Edith's voice rose into the air, 'that the rivers of India join up with the rivers of England? The waters of the lake in which the twins drowned run in deep channels underground and then meet up with rivers which flow to the sea? And when the rivers meet the sea, the souls of Ralph and Grace are carried out into the Indian Ocean and follow the great sea liners all the way to England. They leap with the flying fish and mingle with the spray and are tossed like foam on the crest of the waves. That's why I know that they are here now. Do you understand, Jaspal?' Edith cried urgently. 'Their spirits are here. They came looking for us – I know it.'

Jaspal gazed at the dense surface of this mighty river and felt fear. What powers were contained within its great shining body? What other spirits might they invoke?

'Concentrate on Ralph and Grace! Call them! Call them in your mind! Call them with your voice.'

Edith hung her head over the back of the boat, trying to get her face as close to the surface of the water as she could. 'Ralph! Grace! Do you hear me?' She sounded like a priestess. 'O spirits of the waters, call my brother and sister. Tell them I want to speak to them and ask their forgiveness!'

Edith ceremoniously dipped her arms into the water as she intoned her words. Jaspal dropped the oars into the bottom of the boat and let the craft float free to go wherever it wished. He dragged himself to the prow, and like Edith, heaved himself so far forward that his face too, was nearly in the water and his arms were submerged up to the elbows. He beat at the surface, shouting, 'Ralph! Grace! It's me, Jaspal! Come up from your spirit world and talk to us!'

He gazed at the dark waters, trying to penetrate their depths, trying to make out the flailing limbs once gold, now green, beckoning, reaching, stretching, waving, tangling like weeds; mouths open – breathing, calling, filling up with green water – never again closing.

'Edith!'

'Did you hear that?' Jaspal jerked back on to his knees and looked round. But Edith was still leaning half-out of the boat, face down, her arms trailing in the water while she called out like a loving older sister, 'Ralphie! Gracie! Mummy wants you home now!'

Jaspal looked out across the waters. The moon and clouds mingled with the glistening shadows.

'Edith!' He heard her name again. He jumped to

his feet. 'Edith! They're calling you! I can hear them.' The boat rocked violently, as Edith leapt back and scrambled towards him. 'Jaspal! Jaspal! Edith!' The voices seem to ebb and flow on the wind. High above them, the last of the gulls wheeled about in the night sky.

'Yes, yes, yes!' screamed Edith. 'It's Ralph and Grace. They've come! They've come! I can hear them calling.' She lunged forward and somehow, flew out of the boat with arms outstretched, like wings and, for a second, seemed airborne, gliding miraculously over the surface, but then she hit the water and sank out of sight.

Where was she? Jaspal clutched the sides of the boat, peering out in a panicked frenzy of fear. He couldn't see – it was too dark. Then she bobbed up again, her face as white as the moon; her skirt and blazer ballooning round her, buoying her up as she drifted away with the current.

Jaspal snatched up the oars and began to row. When he was close, he held out an oar for her to grab, but she ignored it, and just floated past him like a princess reclining on her bed, her face pale, hard and as still as a doll's. He tried to keep pace with her, but no matter how hard he thrust the oars into the water, the distance between them gradually lengthened.

A figure was running along the towpath. It was a woman. Her arms were waving. She ran – trying to outdo the current which was carrying Edith away. Suddenly, the woman pulled off her coat and dived into the river. Jaspal saw her fighting through the swirling water, sometimes disappearing, then reappearing again, her arms rising and falling as she thrust her way towards the girl. But, in the darkness, it was impossible to see. Then Jaspal remembered Edith's torch lying between the planks of the boat. He fumbled for it and found it. Desperately he flashed its beam across the waters. Where was she? Then he saw Edith's bobbing head, her hair streaming behind like yellow weeds. The swimmer saw her too in the torchlight and moved into its shining path. At last the woman reached Edith. Her arms lifted above her head like a champion claiming her prize and then she clasped her. Clamping an arm beneath Edith's chin to keep her face out of the water, the woman began to struggle towards the shore. But the current was strong. And though her body struck out in one direction, the current inexorably tugged them further and further away downriver.

Jaspal rowed. He sucked in his breath in a desperate song:

'Heave, heave,
Set the sail and pull the oars and row your way
    to home.
Heave . . . heave . . .'

Back and forth he thrust his body and pulled with all his might upon the oars, trying to break through the powerful waters.

'Heave . . . Heave . . .

Set the sail and pull the oars and row your way
   to home . . .'

It was what the sailors had sung in Bombay as they
worked on the docks or ferried cargo up and down
offshore. He rowed for all he was worth. He no
longer felt his muscles burning with the strain, or
his heart hammering so hard it might leap out of
his chest.

'Jaspal! Jaspal!' He heard his name again, flying
round on the wind, rising above the slap of the
oars. Was it the twins calling or the spirits of
the waters? Again and again the voice called his
name. He stopped rowing and grabbed the torch
and shone it in a wide arc across the surface of the
river. It exposed the woman in the water. She was
close now; her exhausted movements slow and
cumbersome. But her arm was firmly under Edith's
pale face, and with her other arm, she powered
herself nearer and nearer towards Jaspal.

At last her hand reached out and grabbed the
edge of the boat. The boat rocked perilously as she
rested her head with relief against its side. 'Jaspal!'
she sighed.

'Memsahib!' Jaspal gazed down at Edith's
mother.

Out in the darkness, they could hear the chug of
an approaching outboard motor.

*'Marvi my dearest, my precious, my darling!' Jhoti's
voice spoke to her daughter, rippling round her*

brain like a soft song. 'So Mrs Chadwick saved her daughter and proved her love for her.'

'Yes, Ma!' answered Marvinder. 'Jaspal said they clung to each other and would not be parted.'

'You and I were torn apart, were we not, Marvinder, my child? Yet we have not been parted – not for one single day – and we too will come together face to face, will we not?'

'Yes, Ma. We will set out to find you as soon as we can. I promise.'

'What brought the mother to the river?' asked Jhoti.

'Just a feeling,' said Marvinder. 'She had a feeling that she must save her daughter. She ran home from a concert and found that Edith was gone and the boat no longer at its moorings. Something told her. Some instinct.'

'It was the will of the gods,' said Jhoti. 'O Rama Rama Sita Ram!'

FOURTEEN

Sea Change

Locked in his prison cell, Govind began to have a recurring dream. He was in India, cycling down the long white road which ran to his village. The light was bright, dazzling white, and the road ahead of him shimmered in the heat haze. Through the shimmering a young girl, no more than four years old, with a baby clasped to her hip, came running towards him, one arm outstretched in greeting.

He lifted them both on to his crossbar, for they were his children – his daughter Marvinder and his son Jaspal. Now that he had a son, he was strangely keen to see his wife. So he cycled as fast as he could. But when he got to the village, he couldn't find her anywhere.

'Have you seen Jhoti?' he asked. But no one had. Then, suddenly, hobbling towards him, so old that her skin hung from her bones, came Basant, the village midwife. 'Have you seen Jhoti?' he asked her. Then he thought, how foolish I am. How could Basant see Jhoti, when Basant is blind.

But Basant answered, 'Jhoti has gone away to look for you,' and she pointed a claw-like finger westwards towards the sun setting over the fields.

Govind thought he saw a figure in the distance;

150

a woman whose loose tunic and pyjamas fluttered round her body and who clutched a veil to her face.

'Jhoti!' He called her name. The figure turned. 'Jhoti,' he called again, rushing towards her. As he drew near, the figure dropped her veil. Govind stopped dead with terror, for it was then he saw that she had no face.

Each time the dream was as horrible as the last and he would wake up, drenched with fear.

Today, he remembered with relief, was a visitor's day. He looked proudly at the boat he had made for Jaspal. It was a dhow; the sort of boat which people had sailed for thousands of years; the sort of boat in which he knew his grandfather had gone to Africa – a voyage which had lasted about two months, navigating by way of the stars; a simple, deep, open wooden boat, with merely a rudder and some oars; and a tall, curving mast, with one piece of canvas wrapped around it for the sail.

Govind had had to beg and beseech the warders to allow him into the carpentry hall to work, when he had already been assigned to make stuffed toys. But it had enraged him to remember Jaspal saying he was going to make a boat with Billy's father.

He heard the jingle of keys and the clang of doors. His cellmates stirred and groaned. The warders were unlocking them for breakfast. For nearly six months, he had lived in a world of metal – hard, angular, reverberating metal. The doors and bedsteads, the plates from which they ate, the buckets which they slopped out, the metal staircases and landings, rising up through the cage-like building from one railinged and meshed layer to the next – all metal, all ringing and echoing with footsteps and voices, so that he himself felt he had become a metal man, with brains of wire which buzzed in his head till he thought he would go mad.

Only in his dreams at night did he escape into a world of earth and sky; of fire and water. He dreamed of the war: the drone of aeroplanes, the rattle of gunfire and the heart-shaking explosions of bombs. Yet that was the best time, for while the war was on he had mates and comrades. Death did not discriminate between race and colour; and when the noise and clamour of war had swept across his brain, he dreamed of India and his village, Deri. There was the river where he swam, the trees he climbed and the long white road along which he cycled home. There was the gossip of the evening and the card-playing and the sound of children, suddenly made invisible by the rapid descent of darkness. So he had preferred the night to the day, until his dreaming of a faceless Jhoti turned into a nightmare, and the only days he hungered for were the visitors' days.

Today was a visitors' day. As usual, he looked forward to the afternoon, with nervous expectation; full of longing; his eye watched the agonising progress of the clock; his heart beat faster as the hour drew near, and his palms sweated with anticipation. He made up so many speeches in his head; he would tell Jaspal this and Marvinder that. He would make it up to Maeve and be a better father to Beryl.

152

Yet, as the time went by, his thoughts turned increasingly to Jhoti. The wrong he had done her weighed inside him like a heavy lump, which time only increased rather than diminished. He needed to know if she was alive. He needed her forgiveness.

Govind entered the visitors' hall, proudly carrying the wooden boat. He rapidly scanned the room. He looked only for Jaspal's turbaned head, and so, at first, he failed to see Harold Chadwick sitting at a table. Then he couldn't help a sigh of disappointment and the gleam went out of his eye.

Harold Chadwick got up and greeted him – more awkwardly than usual, Govind thought, for he barely looked him in the eye. They sat down simultaneously with the boat placed between them. Harold leaned forward and admired it, then began talking rapidly, as if the faster he talked, the quicker he would get it over with.

'Govind, I have been asked by the O'Grady family to give you some news.'

Govind saw the solemnity of Harold's face and gripped the table with alarm. 'Oh God! It's not my children? Jaspal? Has something bad happened to Jaspal?'

'No, no, no. It's nothing like that. The children are in good form. It's Maeve.' Harold looked at him gently. 'She's left you. She's gone to America with some GI she met and fell in love with. She's taken Beryl too.' Harold paused, allowing the information to sink in.

They sat in silence for a long time, then Govind

said, half to himself, 'I wonder if she took the horse.'

'What horse?' asked Harold.

'The one I made for Marvinder, but I gave it to Beryl, I don't know why. I was proud of it. It was a bridegroom's horse. I managed to get all sorts of scraps of material to decorate it – even bits of silver and gold thread. Maeve said she would give it to her. I hope so, because then Beryl will always remember me every time she sees the horse.' He dropped his head on his hands. There was another long pause.

Then Harold was talking; he was being practical, explaining arrangements, but Govind hardly heard him. He breathed in and out. Everyone receded. He felt he was floating in space. A cord had been cut, and he wasn't sure in which direction he would go. He didn't feel anything. Not grief, nor joy. Then he said slowly, 'Does that make me free? Free to go back to India?' He fingered the dhow as he spoke, rubbing his thumb along the smooth sides he had so carefully planed.

'Well, yes, it does. Which brings me to the next thing I want to discuss with you if you're up to it,' said Harold, pulling his chair closer in a practical manner. 'Look here, Govind, I have good news too. Especially in the circumstances. The missionaries from the Deri area have been approached for help in reconstructing the village school – your school and mine. It was destroyed during Partition. They want me to go back and get it back on its feet. I've had a number of meetings with the Mission Centre

154

in London and made it clear that I must be able to put in local staff and train them to take over. They said there was already one man on the spot – you may know him. A man called Bahadhur Manmohan Singh. He's probably some years younger than you. Anyway, I suggested you be taken on as well.'

'Me?' Govind echoed weakly. 'Who would look at an ex-con?' he sighed, tears welling up in his eyes.

'They had their reservations, I won't deny it,' said Harold. 'But I told them I had known you since you were a boy. I knew that you were the most talented pupil I had taught, and that you were ruined by the war in Europe – a war which was not of your making, and yet one in which you nobly enlisted and fought on our side. I said they owed it to you to give you a second chance. Finally, they agreed. You'll probably have to have a short refresher course first, but then, you will be able to take up a position back in Deri at your own school. What do you think of that, eh, Govind? Start a new life back home? Maeve has gone. Your marriage was never valid – either by law or in the eyes of your religion or hers. She will remarry and start a completely new life. You must too. What do you say?'

Govind breathed and closed his eyes. 'Jhoti! How many lives do I have?' he murmured. The long white road shimmered into view.

'Did your father make a horse for me, Marvinder, my dearest? A bridal horse – with an embroidered

155

saddle and gold threads plaited in its tail, and bells threaded into its mane, and garlands of marigolds and jasmine hanging from the reins?'

'Yes, ma. He made a beautiful horse. But he gave it to Beryl – and now Beryl's run away with her mother. They've gone to America with an American soldier.'

'Did they take the horse?'

'Yes, Ma, they did.'

'Oh!' The long sigh died with disappointment.

Maeve and Beryl had gone. It was as though the ground had opened up and taken them both, there seemed so little trace of them.

Marvinder and Kathleen had come home from school. Kathleen noticed straight away that something was different. Usually, Beryl would have been playing on the front step – that was the first indication. The front door was shut, when it was usually wide open. There were no toys scattered about the hall and her rusty old pushchair was not anywhere to be seen. Worst of all, there was a strange silence.

'Maeve! Beryl?' Kathleen had yelled up the stairway. There was no answer. She went bounding up two at a time, dashing first into her flat on the first floor. 'Mum! Are you there?'

But Mrs O'Grady was out and as the big black pram was missing, they knew she was collecting laundry.

Kathleen called out again, as she climbed up to Maeve's flat on the second floor. But no one answered. She opened the door. It wasn't locked. She stepped inside, quietly, as if going into a church. Marvinder, who had followed her all the way, stood at her shoulder. 'They've gone out!'

Yet even as they stood there, staring round Maeve's room, they could see something was different. It was too tidy. Maeve wasn't a particularly tidy person. She often left the washing-up in the sink and bundles of clothes lying around. But today everything seemed put away. Kathleen walked over to the dressing-table. It was bare. Where were all the tubes of lipstick and bottles of nail varnish?

'Oh my God!' Kathleen's hand flew to her mouth as she was struck by a thought. 'I wonder if they've been burgled and kidnapped. Look, Marvi! Everything's gone.'

Kathleen began pulling open all the drawers. Empty, empty, empty! She rushed over to Beryl's cot. Empty. Just old blankets, outgrown clothes, some nappies, laddered stockings and worn-out shoes. Everything else had gone.

Kathleen's breath sucked in and out noisily. 'Oh blessed saints! Oh Mary, Mother of God! Where's Mammy? Where's Da? We must go and find them. We'd better go to the police.' Frantically, she flew down the stairs again, Marvinder close behind, and at that moment, Mrs O'Grady appeared, struggling backwards up the front steps, heaving the big black pram which was full of washing.

'Mammy! Thank God you've come!' Kathleen was almost crying now. 'It's Maeve and Beryl.

They've been robbed and kidnapped. They've vanished – and almost everything they own as well!'

Mrs O'Grady would have let go the pram had not Marvinder grabbed it and helped her to heave it to the top step.

The door of Ground Floor Flat Number 1 flew open, and Mrs Beard leered at them maliciously. 'If it's Maeve you're looking for, I saw her go off in a taxi like a proper lady. She took that half . . .' she corrected herself meaningfully '. . . her little girl with her, and a couple of suitcases. Gone away, has she?' Her question hung in the air with spiteful innocence.

With a stifled cry, Mrs O'Grady stumbled up the stairs followed by Kathleen. Marvinder stayed below. Mrs Beard continued to gawp at her with gleeful hostility, then slammed the door. Marvinder pulled the abandoned pram further into the hall-way, then stood waiting and listening. A terrible sense of foreboding overwhelmed her. She heard Kathleen and her mother clattering wildly up to the top floor and go into Maeve's flat. After a while they thudded down again to the O'Grady flat. She heard Mrs O'Grady give an exclamation. 'What's this!' Then there was a long silence. She heard Kathleen plead, 'What is it, Ma? Is it from Maeve? What does she say?'

Softly, almost on tiptoe, Marvinder climbed the stairs. As she neared the top, she peered between the banister railings, through the open door into the flat. Mrs O'Grady was flopped at the kitchen table clutching a letter, while Kathleen stood behind with her hands on her mother's shoulders. As Marvinder entered, Mrs O'Grady looked up eagerly, as if hoping it was Maeve, then sank back in despair.

'Shall we call the police?' asked Marvinder in a small voice.

Kathleen shook her head.

'What's happened? Is it bad?'

'Maeve's gone and run off with an American GI called Ricky. She's taken Beryl. They're going to America!'

As each member of the family came home, they read the letter and each had their own reaction. Mr O'Grady stormed and bellowed, cursing and swearing; first he called Maeve everything under the sun, then suddenly, he aimed his fury at Govind. 'We were all right till that coolie came along, flashing his teeth and seducing our Maeve . . .' His anger and language got worse and worse.

Jaspal came home from school to find Marvinder sitting on the wall outside, where she had fled from Mr O'Grady's torrent of rage. 'They're blaming Pa,' she stammered, after she had told Jaspal what had happened. Jaspal sat on the wall next to her. They waited, unsure what to do. They could hear Mr O'Grady ranting and raging. The whole street could hear. 'Well, that Govind can go to blazes now, and take his brats with him. I don't want to see hair nor hide of them ever again . . .'

'Does he mean we can't live here any more?' cried Jaspal.

159

'I don't know. Perhaps he doesn't mean it.' Marvinder tried to sound reassuring.

It was nearly six before Michael and Patrick came roaring up on their motorbike, all covered in building-site dust.

'What are you two doing out here, sitting like a couple of garden gnomes?' asked Michael.

'Anything wrong?' Patrick enquired, suddenly noticing their solemn faces, and Marvinder close to tears.

'It's Maeve and Beryl . . .' She tried to speak, but the words got choked up in her throat.

'They've run off to America with some bloke.' Jaspal finished it off for her.

'They WHAT?' Michael shouted.

'I knew it!' exploded Patrick. 'I saw her making sheep's eyes at that Yankee fellow. I warned her about it. My God . . . the stupid girl . . .'

'It's that Ricky fellow, isn't it? The one at the Hammersmith Palais. He gave her cigarettes and nylon stockings. I told her she shouldn't 'ave accepted them, but she's a wild one, our Maeve. I saw how she danced with him . . . and he was there every time we went these last weeks . . . I bloomin' well warned that Yank she was a married woman with a kiddie . . . Jeezuz Mary . . . if I ever catch up with him . . .'

The two brothers leapt the front steps and went racing up the stairs. Soon their voices, too, came blasting out of the window as everyone accused everyone else.

'Trouble, is there?' Dr Silbermann came out of

160

the basement flat and looked sympathetically at Jaspal and Marvinder still huddled on the wall, too scared to move.

Marvinder nodded.

'Do you want to come down to me?' he asked kindly.

Marvinder nodded again and, pulling Jaspal with her off the wall, gratefully followed Dr Silbermann into the quiet calm of his flat.

He didn't ask any questions, just put on the kettle and made them all a cup of tea. Then he went to the cupboard and got out a brown paper bag. It was full of broken biscuits. 'Would you like one?' he offered.

'Thanks!' breathed Jaspal, dipping in his hand and clutching at two or three.

'Don't be greedy,' hissed Marvinder, but then found two or three just slipped into her hand too. They were terribly hungry. They stuffed them into their mouths, rubbing their sleeves across their faces to brush off the crumbs.

'Hmmm,' murmured Dr Silbermann. 'Perhaps I'd better give you something more substantial. How about I poach you a couple of eggs?' He went to the cupboard again and took out another paper bag in which there were three eggs. He was just taking out two, when there was a discreet knock on the door. Carefully, he put the eggs on the table among the pots of varnish and bottles of spirit and went to see who it was.

''Ave you got Jaspal and Marvi?' It was Kathleen. She looked pale and strained. She gazed past Dr

Silbermann and saw Jaspal and Marvinder sunk into his sofa among all the papers and manuscripts. 'You're to come and 'ave your tea,' she said bluntly.

Marvinder glanced at Dr Silbermann. He smiled encouragingly. 'Well, that's good. You'd better run along then, both of you. Perhaps you can have tea with me another time.'

Jaspal and Marvinder followed Kathleen upstairs. When they entered the O'Gradys' flat everything looked normal – and yet, wasn't normal. Mr O'Grady was sitting as usual by the fireplace, cigarette in hand, with his good leg up on the mantelpiece. Mrs O'Grady was busy at the kitchen stove stirring a saucepan of stew. Michael stooped over the kitchen sink washing himself down, while Patrick crouched at a table in the corner, tuning in the wireless.

Nobody turned to greet them as they came in. Nobody was speaking. Kathleen left them standing just in the doorway and went over to Patrick. 'Is it time for *ITMA*?' she asked.

'Soon. Ten minutes.'

Suddenly there was a clatter of plates as Mrs O'Grady prepared to serve the stew. Mr O'Grady lifted his leg off the mantelpiece and heaved himself to a standing position with the help of his crutches. Michael finished towelling himself dry, hastily put a comb through his hair, then came to the table. Patrick and Kathleen came over and sat down, but Jaspal and Marvinder didn't move.

Patrick said quietly, 'Come on, you two. Come and have your tea.'

162

Maeve and Beryl's departure had been so unexpected; so final. There had been no farewells. It was as if they had both died and yet no one had seen the bodies, so it was hard to take it in. One minute they were there – the next gone, taking everything they could in two suitcases. There was only the note Maeve had left on the kitchen table.

'. . . I didn't want to tell you because you would have persuaded me to stay. But my mind was made up. I wasn't really married to Govind, so now I can marry Ricky. He's a plumber back home in Ohio and hopes to run his own business. We'll live in a house. He doesn't mind Beryl. It's my one chance for a new life – and I'm taking it . . . '

But ever since then, everyone had been short-tempered. Mrs O'Grady cried and fumed and yelled and threatened, and then went silent and took to her bed for three days. Mr O'Grady swung his crutch at anyone who got on his nerves – particularly Jaspal and Marvinder. 'That father of yours better stay in prison for the next twenty years. He'll be safer there, I can tell you, because if I get my hands on him, I'll bash his brains out . . .' He swore and cursed and thumped the table. Even Kathleen had gone quiet. She missed Maeve and Beryl terribly. She cried a lot and rejected any comfort Marvinder tried to give her.

Govind was held responsible for all Maeve's woes and her departure. It was all because of Govind that things had come to such a pass. They would never forgive him. Suddenly, Govind was no longer part of the household.

For a while, life continued: Jaspal and Marvinder went to school each day; Marvinder did the paper round with Kathleen and tried to continued practising her violin. But it made Mr O'Grady furious. Although she had retreated to the boys' bedroom, it still annoyed him.

Doh re mi fa so la ti doh – Marvinder always practised her scales, up and down and up another octave, changing the position, and trying to place her fingers down on the string with absolute accuracy. If she was a little off-key, she tried again and again until she got it right, and then went on to the next scale.

'For pity's sake! Can't you stop that terrible racket? It's getting on me nerves,' bellowed Mr O'Grady, thumping a crutch on the floor.

Marvinder lowered her bow helplessly. What could she do? She needed to practise. The Music Festival was coming up. She shuddered with fright at the thought of it.

'Oh calm down, you'll burst a blood vessel,' she heard Mrs O'Grady intervene.

'Calm down, calm down,' he echoed sneeringly. 'I bloody well won't calm down. What's to become of them two, I'd like to know? What are we doing with that good-for-nothing's brats – what with that barbarian, Jaspal, messing about getting into fist fights and playing truant, and her caterwauling on that piece of wood all day. I don't know why we ever took them on in the first place. It's your soft heart what did it, Mother,' he now turned on his wife, blaming her for everything.

Marvinder put her violin away. She looked as if she was going to faint. Patrick had come home just then. He saw her face and was suddenly kind. He came up and held her elbow and protested at his father's cruel words. 'Hey, Da! Shut it with your blathering. Why take it out on these two? They're innocent.'

'Huh! Innocent, my foot! I'm the one who's innocent. I never asked for all this rubbish – and after what I did in the war, losing my leg and all that. And what's my reward?' Mr O'Grady snorted furiously. When nobody answered, he shouted, 'I'm off to the pub, and I won't be coming back till I'm riproaring drunk!' and he crashed and banged his way out of the house.

'Don't you go minding now what that old devil has to say,' said Patrick giving her a squeeze. 'Just get on with your practising, now that he's at the pub.'

'When are you going into the Navy?' asked Marvinder, wishing he would go on holding her elbow for ever.

'Couple of weeks.'

'Will you be there when I play at the festival?'

'You have to win first, isn't that what you said?' He grinned teasingly.

'And if I do, will you?' she asked, blushing.

'You bet I'll be there. I wouldn't miss a lesson in Truth and Beauty for anything. I don't think I'll be getting much of that in the Navy.'

'Oh, but the sea is beautiful!' cried Marvinder. 'I watched it for hours – and days. There was always something about it. The way it gathered itself up and heaved and fell, all the patterns swirling and the colours changing – especially from blue and green when the sky was blue and the sun shone all day, to grey and black as we neared England. When you've been at sea for days and days, with sea all around, nothing is more exciting than standing at the railing waiting to see land. It starts as a smudge. You're not sure if it's the blurred horizon or the way the light falls, but you keep looking and looking and gradually it becomes more solid . . .' she trailed off, laughing. 'You think I'm daft, don't you?'

He let go of her elbow. 'Will you miss me, Marvi?'

'Oh yes. I will,' Marvinder cried passionately, though she wondered if he had heard her. He was already looking past her to the door. 'It won't be the same without all your caterwauling,' he teased, giving her plaits a playful tug. Then he yelled for his brother. 'Hey, Michael. You coming down the Feathers? I'm parched!'

'Wish I could join the Army or the Navy,' yelled Jaspal, passing them on the stairs. 'I want to learn to kill.'

Rama and Sita were banished into the forest for fourteen years. In such a situation, everyone suffers; those who are banished and loved ones who are left behind. But you can be banished from people's hearts too – and that can be worse than a jungle.'

'I don't know what will become of us, Ma,' cried Marvinder.

FIFTEEN

Hanuman

'Hanuman . . . Hanuman . . . Hanuman . . .' Jaspal and his gang chanted low and menacingly. They clenched their fists and grated their teeth. They adjusted their bandanas round their heads and clustered round Jaspal.

They were going to the tracks. It was a place where several railway lines converged, criss-crossing through signals and points, like a nest of serpents, whose shining, writhing bodies snaked away through the derelict wasteland. There were pits and bomb craters, rubble and broken train sheds. These were the hiding places and battlegrounds of rival gangs.

Jaspal had looked strange when he met up with his followers. He wore his black turban and his eyes glittered with a kind of repressed fury. They felt the anger almost crackling in his body; its force touched them and made them brace themselves. Tonight they were going to fight Johnnie Cudlip's Spitfire gang. There was danger in the air – and fear. They chanted even louder, to quell the terror rising in their guts, and they jostled closer together, trying to pool whatever courage each had, to make

167

it more powerful. 'Hanuman... Hanuman... Hanuman...'

They moved rapidly through the back streets and down the darkened alleyways. The moon followed them overhead like a giant eye, watching them; casting shadows for them to merge into when needed, or providing a low beam to guide their way as they came nearer the sidings, where the street lamps no longer cast their light.

They approached from the south, staying this side of the tracks, knowing that the Spitfires would come from the north. They fanned out, picking a place to hide and watch; some crouched in the craters or lay flat on their stomachs behind broken walls; others climbed up perilously onto the blasted roofs of the train sheds. They hid in twos and threes, each wondering if his hammering heart could be heard by the others. Each knew the different signals; three soft hoots through cupped hands, as soon as any movement was detected over the tracks; a screech, like the sound of a hunting owl, which could be made by stretching a blade of grass between the thumbs and blowing – this meant danger; and a series of whistles was a means of checking that everyone was all right and in position.

Jaspal moved free. He was Hanuman, who could change himself into anything. First he was the scout, then a spy. He liked to run, invisible, and get into enemy lines. He wore his plimsolls so that he could move silently and, thinking himself a cat, sidled into his opponent's domain, watching and listening, his brain working out strategies. He sped across the tracks into enemy territory and found a vantage point. It was a broken signal post. Now he was a monkey, able to shin up to the top and sit astride the metal arm. From here he could look all around with a cunning eye.

He saw a flash of white shirt just ducking into a shed. Then he saw dark shapes, running, low as wolves. They were coming. Gripping the post with his knees, he freed his hands, so that he could cup them together and hoot out a warning. He saw the shapes halt and listen, then they were off again, disappearing finally into a series of hiding places.

Suddenly he saw Johnnie Cudlip. He knew it was Johnnie because he was taller than the rest. The sight of him brought his anger sizzling to the surface. Jaspal wanted a fight. His desire to fight made him rash. Mercilessly, he watched Johnnie take up a hiding place, crouched behind the wheels of an abandoned goods truck, which had been pushed up a siding. Jaspal wanted to laugh out loud. He descended from his perch, hardly feeling the splinters in his hands as he slid back down the signal post. He plucked a blade of grass and stretched it between his thumbs. He was about to send the warning to his gang members, when he stopped. There was time to bring them all out. First, he wanted to taunt Johnnie; put the wind up him; make him look stupid.

He crept stealthily towards the goods truck and then circled it, so that he could come up behind Johnnie. He picked up some stones and tossed one over to the left. Johnnie swung round to look, and

169

Jaspal tossed another stone over to the right. Jonny looked there. 'Who is it?' he hissed. 'Is that you, Bernie?' Jaspal sniggered out loud and crept underneath the truck as Johnnie jumped up with alarm.

Johnnie put three fingers in his mouth and gave an earth-shattering whistle. There came a number of answering whistles, and a flurry of scuffling feet as a number of his gang appeared.

'What's up, Johnnie?' they hissed.

'I dunno, I heard something,' whispered Johnnie looking around. He didn't like to say what he had heard in case he looked stupid. 'Anyone seen any sign of the Hanumans?'

'No, Johnnie!'

'Well, you, Bernie, and you, Dave, Mick and Roy, get out there and see if they've come. You take the route by the old engine, Dave and Mick go by the signal box. Roy, get the others to get in line along the tracks. Let's be ready for them.'

Jaspal lay motionless. He was only centimetres away from them. He laughed inwardly; he would never let them live this down. There were were discussing their plans right in front of him. How he would flaunt their words at them – once he had got away to safety. He must just choose his moment to get back to his own side of the track and alert his gang. He lay there on his stomach, his chin cupped on his arms, when suddenly, he heard a faint scurrying. Jaspal looked up. Staring at him, centimetres from his face, were the beady, vicious eyes of a large rat.

'AAAaaaaaaah.' Jaspal tried to stifle his scream,

but he couldn't. It was a bloodcurdling scream which emptied his lungs and echoed all round the sidings. It was a scream so terrible, so full of horror, that it brought Jaspal's gang scrambling out of their hiding-places and Johnnie's gang rushing about like frightened chickens. Jaspal rolled out from under the truck and began to run. There was so much confusion that, in the darkness, Jaspal would have got away, had it not been for a passenger train which suddenly came down the track. Every carriage was lit up and a great beam on the front of the engine exposed the whole area. There he was, caught in the strobing light of the passing train, his silhouette unmistakable and his escape blocked.

'Yeah!' A cry of triumph went up from Johnnie's gang. 'Get 'im, get 'im, get 'im!' they chanted. They converged upon him from all sides, while Jaspal's gang could only wait helplessly for the train to pass.

When finally it had gone, the Hanumans stood on their side of the track, bewildered and scared. The great beaming light of the train had vanished and left them in a deep darkness; even the moon seemed to have abandoned them. There was no sound. They couldn't see anyone or hear anything. Instinctively, the gang gathered round Billy. As Jaspal's best friend, he was second-in-command.

'What do we do?' they whispered nervously.

'Have they killed him?'

'Billy, what do we do?'

'I don't know, I don't know. Let me think, will you?' Then Billy somehow knew that there was only one thing they could do, other than run like lily-livered cowards. Softly, he began to chant. 'Hanuman . . . Hanuman . . . Hanuman . . . Hanuman . . .' The others took it up. The more they chanted it, the braver they felt. They turned in one body and began to advance across the track, moving in rhythm. 'Hanuman . . . Hanuman . . . Hanuman . . .'

'Oi! You lot!' It was Johnnie.

They didn't stop, but carried on chanting as they moved forward. 'Hanuman . . . Hanuman . . . Hanuman . . .' They were across the railway lines now, into enemy territory. They quickened up the chant. 'Hanuman, Hanuman, Hanuman!'

Johnnie's voice yelled out again. 'We've got your Hanuman! We have your leader! He's our prisoner, so shut up if you want him back!'

The sound of chanting died away fretfully. 'You'd better not hurt him, Johnnie!' yelled Billy, sounding as threatening as he could.

'Oh yeah? And what will you do about it?' jeered Johnnie.

'Jaspal, are you all right?' shouted Billy.

There was no answer. Maybe he had got away. Perhaps it was all a trick and Johnnie hadn't got him at all. Billy started up the chanting again. 'Hanuman, Hanuman, Hanuman . . .'

Suddenly someone cried, 'Hey look!' There, up on the roof of a derelict shed, was Jaspal. He was gripped by several boys, who twisted his arms behind his back. Two boys had torches which they shone in his face, causing him to be blinded. Then Johnnie appeared on the roof. He shook a box of matches and struck one of them. 'I'll make a deal with you,' he said. 'I don't want us to be enemies. Surrender, and swear to join my gang.'

'Never,' shouted Billy. 'Never,' shouted the others.

'You think this bandage-head is so great, do you? Don't you realise he's our prisoner? There's no girly-wirly to save him now. We can do anything we like with him – can't we boys?'

'Yeah, yeah, yeah!' his gang chanted triumphantly. 'Kill, kill, kill!'

'Shall we kill him?'

'Yeah!' they bellowed, ecstatically.

'You know what!' cried Johnnie. 'I think killing's too good for him. We'll humiliate him. We'll show him what happens if a bandage-head meddles with us.' He struck another match and then tugged at Jaspal's turban. With a yell of triumph, he pulled and pulled, while his gang twirled their captive round and round like a top, squealing with mirth, as his turban unravelled. Part of the turban was still wound round his head, when Johnny struck another match and held it to the end of the thin material. There was a sizzling sound.

Billy and Jaspal's gang groaned in horror.

Suddenly the whole turban flared. Jonny and his gang fell back, disconcerted by the speed at which the fire took hold.

'Hey, put it out, Johnnie,' someone cried. But it was too late. Within seconds, the turban was ablaze, and they just stood helplessly watching.

Laughing like a maniac, Jaspal ripped the rest of

the turban off his head and, still holding the end in one hand, he began to leap at Johnnie and his gang, whirling the flaming material round and round, thrusting it at them. 'Hanuman ... Hanuman ... Hanuman ...' he shrieked.

Jumping, falling, tumbling, Johnnie and his gang threw themselves from the shed, anything to get away as Jaspal lunged at them with the burning turban. He jumped down after them. Billy and the rest of Jaspal's gang moved in and soon there were struggling bodies punching, kicking and rolling around, while Jaspal pranced in and out of the fray, swirling the fiery turban like a comet. Then, he came face to face with Johnnie. They stared at each other.

'Go on, run away, little boy,' Jaspal mocked him and flicked the burning ends of the turban at him, trying to make him flinch. Johnnie stood his ground, leering back at him. With a roar of rage, Jaspal flung himself onto his enemy, trying to envelop him with the turban, not caring that he himself was caught in the flames.

There was the sound of a police siren. The two gangs fled, stumbling away in all directions. Billy leapt on Jaspal, pulling him away. 'It's the police, Jaspal. Come on! Let's get away.' But, already, helmeted figures came running towards them.

Some days later, when Kathleen and Marvinder got back from the paper round, it was to find Mrs O'Grady waiting at the door, with two packed suitcases and Marvinder's violin. Jaspal was dressed and standing motionless in the hall, his hands still bandaged from the burns.

'Who's going, Mammy?' asked Kathleen.

'Them two,' she said harshly. Then her voice softened when she saw Marvinder's stricken face. 'Look, no hard feelings, eh? You're a good child, but I can't manage him. He's become such a handful – and it was so shaming the way he was brought back in a police car. They said it was a terrible fight. Lucky no one was killed. We can't do nothing more with him.' She indicated Jaspal with a jerk of her head. 'Someone else must try. You've no place here now. You don't belong with us no more – not now that Maeve's gone. There's no blood shared between us. When your da gets out, he won't be coming here neither. We'll not be having nothing more to do with any of you.'

'Where are we going?' whispered Marvinder, filled with dread.

'I've fixed it all up. I phoned them posh friends of yours, the Chadwicks. He'll be around any minute. You're going to live with them now. I told them, I can't manage any more – especially not with Mr O'Grady being so dead against it. Your da's going to be coming out soon, perhaps he'll be able to sort out Jaspal. Anyway, now with Maeve and Beryl gone, what would be the sense in him or you living here? Don't you see?'

Marvinder looked down Whitworth Road. It seemed to blur and turn into the long white road as she last saw it, stretching out before her, filled end to end with creaking bullock carts, and piled

175

with refugees and their belongings. They were refugees again. She had learned to call Mrs O'Grady 'Mam', and Kathleen had been like a sister to her; and as for Beryl, why had everyone forgotten that Beryl was her sister too? They shared the same blood. Did Marvinder, too, not grieve at her departure? She had delighted in having a real sister – even though she knew that, as much as she loved Beryl, Jaspal hated her. Beryl only reminded him of their father's betrayal. But Beryl was gone. Perhaps they would never see her ever again.

Marvinder felt as if she were sinking under the sea. Her body was being carried away, out of control. Questions tumbled over and over in her mind. What about school? What about Dr Silbermann? What about Michael and Patrick – Patrick... would she ever see him again?

'Are we never to see you?' she stammered.

'Oh, Marvi!' Kathleen suddenly flung her arms round her. 'Must she go, Mammy? Why must she go? Who'll do the paper round with me? It's bad enough Maeve and Beryl going, why must Marvi go? Jaspal won't fight no more. Please, Mam!'

'Shut it, Kathy!' muttered Mrs O'Grady roughly. 'It's for the best.'

Harold Chadwick's car turned into Whitworth Road.

Marvinder made as if to dash away into the house, but Mrs O'Grady stopped her. 'Look, my pet, don't make it harder,' she said with sudden gentleness. 'I've packed everything, I promise. And perhaps you'll visit us one day – when all this has died down a bit.'

Marvinder looked up at the grimy windows. Mr O'Grady had been watching them, but drew away as she glanced up. Patrick and Michael would be at work now. She wondered if they knew. 'What about Patrick?' she couldn't help crying out.

'Patrick's off into the Navy soon. We'll all be missing Patrick.'

Mr Chadwick tried to be jovial as he piled their cases into the boot, then opened the passenger doors for them. 'On the move again, eh? Edith's thrilled you're coming to live with us for a while.'

Jaspal hadn't said a word. He jerked away from Mrs O'Grady when she tried to pat his back, and he wouldn't say 'goodbye'.

When the car reached the top of the road, Marvinder looked back. Kathleen and Mrs O'Grady were still standing there, watching as if they would stand for ever. Then the car turned the corner and they were gone.

'Marvinder ... where ... where are you?' Her *mother's voice sounded more urgent.*

'We're here in Richmond, living with the Chadwicks. They didn't want us in Whitworth Road any more.'

'The Chadwicks ... oh!' Jhoti's voice softened with remembrance. 'When I worked at the Chadwicks ... I would take the path from our village at dawn, just before the sun had struck the rim of our horizon; when the only sound was the cock

crowing and Iqbal, the tailor, calling out his morning prayers as he bowed towards Mecca.

'I used to imagine I was a snake sliding silently towards the Chadwicks' bungalow. I always hoped I could leave my husband's house before anyone else had woken, for they all detested me working for the memsahib. They were jealous, you know. They would have liked to keep me imprisoned in the kitchen where they could beat me if they chose. After all, I was the youngest wife of the youngest son, even if he was such a high-up, over in Europe. How my other sisters-in-law hated seeing me going to the mission bungalow. They kicked and pinched me whenever they had the chance. Just because Govind was away in England and there was no one to stand up for me, they thought they could treat me as they liked – as if I were a slave. I would have gone mad if I had not been able to escape to the Chadwicks.

'I'd go to the kitchen where old Shanta was moving sleepily around preparing the tray for bed tea. Already the metal lid of the kettle was jiggling up and down as the water boiled and steamed. Old Shanta needed two hands to lift it and pour a quivering cataract of liquid into the huge china teapot. Shanta's hands were not so steady these days, so it was I who would carry the tray to the sahib and memsahib. I would knock softly on their door and call out, "Bed tea"! Still feeling like a snake, I would glide into their darkened room. First the memsahib's hand would creep out from under the mosquito net and draw in the cup; then, from *the other side, the sahib did the same. My next task was to open the shutters and mesh windows where the mosquitoes would be gathering, whining to be let out into the light of day. Is that how it is with you, my daughter?'*

'A little bit, Ma! But it is Mr Chadwick who makes bed tea every morning and takes it into Mrs Chadwick; and they don't sleep under mosquito nets in England.'

SIXTEEN

A Woman in the Jungle

In England, April sees the end of spring and the beginning of summer. That's why poets love it. It is capricious and unreliable, like an animal, not quite wild and not quite tame. Its moods change, not just day by day, but sometimes hour by hour. It isn't really cold, not winter cold, and yet it isn't hot either. And so the people who live in these islands are always trying to judge and foretell what the day will be like – and will they need a brolly or a cardy or a coat or a mac? And often land up carrying everything, just in case.

But one thing is certain; in every crack and crevice and nook and cranny – of walls, houses, pavement stones and roads, whether tended by man or left to fend for themselves – seeds have blown in on the wind and secretly settled, just waiting ... waiting ... for the awakening. Then there is riot and invasion and you know, that if Man weren't there to control it, even those vast stone cities would disappear beneath an onslaught of trees, saplings, grasses, weeds and glorious, glorious flowers of every colour – and once more, Nature would rule all-powerful. That is April in England.

But in India, on the Punjab plain, the heat has

built up and up through February and March, and April is the month of the harvest. Already the wheat is turning to gold and the barley swelling and the mustard flower burning your eyes; and the mangoes are ripening on the tree and bananas bunching, so heavy that the stems on which they hang bend with the weight. High-nosed camels plod their tracks round and round the water wells. All day long, they pull a paternoster of dripping water cans, which clank their way ten metres up and empty themselves, one after the other, into a series of irrigation channels. From here, the water injects itself into the fields, running like silver threads, glistening among the crops.

Far from this scene of cultivation, a white horse steps through the jungle. It follows tracks which feel firm to the hoof, and avoids overhanging creepers and trailing branches. It winds its way through the dense, green foliage, ignoring the shrill gibbering of monkeys and the sharp barking of the fox; it barely startles the dappled buck deer, grazing in the undergrowth, or the turquoise peacock trailing across its path.

The two boys who huddle on the horse's back, make no effort to guide it. The older one knows that somewhere, in a deep, shady hollow, the tiger would be sleeping, and that, in many a great-limbed tree, the leopard had slung its weary body after a night of hunting. In such a wilderness, better to let an animal's instinct be the guide. So Bublu leans his head on Sparrow's shoulder, who in turn slumps forward over the horse's mane, his arms clasped loosely round its neck, and they allow themselves to be carried wherever the horse wills.

It was just before the sun had reached its burning zenith, and the whole jungle steamed with heat, that the horse came to a shallow river. It picked its way along the bank until it reached the water's edge and here it stopped and dropped its head to drink, causing the dozing Sparrow to tumble straight down its neck to the ground. Bublu laughed and swung himself off the horse's back, leaping down beside the child.

Sparrow suddenly backed away from him with terror. 'Is it true what One Eye said? Are you a Muslim? Are you going to kill me?' he stuttered.

'O ye of little faith!' Bublu laughed scornfully. 'Have I not been your friend and protector? Have I not carried you? Shared my food with you, comforted you at night when your dreams terrified you? Have I not been mother and father to you, and sister and brother? Why would you believe the word of a cheat and a bully rather than me, eh, Sparrow?' He turned angrily and flung himself into the water, submerging completely. He seemed to be under a long time. Sparrow got slowly to his feet with alarm, watching for Bublu to emerge. Then suddenly Bublu burst to the surface with a great whoosh, all dripping and glistening as he washed and drank all at the same time.

Sparrow was ashamed. He hung his head and sidled along the shore.

'Hey, don't go too far!' warned Bublu.

Sparrow burst into tears. 'I'm sorry, I'm sorry,

I'm sorry!' he repeated desperately over and over again. 'Please forgive me, Bublu. Please don't stop being my friend!'

Bublu sprang out of the water and rushed up to Sparrow. He grabbed him by an arm and a leg and hurled him into the river, then jumped in after him. For a long time they played and splashed, their laughter echoing through the forest, while the white horse sauntered along the shore, nibbling at the bushes and flicking his long creamy tail to keep at bay the cloud of insects which hovered over him.

It was only when they finally flopped exhausted upon some boulders, that Bublu realised they were being observed.

'Look!' he breathed with quiet anxiety.

Sparrow huddled fearfully up to Bublu. Over on the far shore, it watched them, the wild child. Jungli had always terrified Sparrow – and never more than now, as he crouched, deadly, like a beast sizing up its prey.

The wild child gave a low whistle, and the white horse immediately ambled into the river, crossing the shallows to the other side.

Jungli grasped the horse's mane and with a light spring was instantly on its back. The horse turned into the undergrowth. As he did, the wild child looked over his shoulder at the boys as if to beckon them.

'We must follow,' whispered Bublu, leaping to his feet.

'No, no! It's probably a demon. It will surely kill us,' stammered Sparrow.

'It's not a demon – it's a boy – barely older than yourself. The teacher said so. Anyway, we have no choice,' stated Bublu firmly. 'We are hours into the jungle. I've no idea which way to go to get out. We could get eaten by tigers or stung by snakes. We must follow them. Come! Quickly,' and heaving Sparrow onto his hip, Bublu plunged into the river and crossed to the other side.

There was a barely definable track along which the horse and the wild child must have gone, for the jungle grew as thick as a fortress on either side of it, and there was no sign of any disturbance in the undergrowth. So Bublu followed the path, jogging steadily until he caught a glimpse of the white flanks of the horse moving smoothly ahead. Bublu slowed down to a walking pace and dropped Sparrow to the ground to ease his aching arms.

'Walk a bit. They won't go far from us now,' panted Bublu.

After a while, they realised that the ground was rising. Trees balanced on the edge of rocky hillocks, their whole root systems exposed like the beamed roofs of underground cathedrals. There were giant trees, with vast trunks rising up, universes in themselves, on which all sorts of life forms depended; creepers and suckers, climbers and parasites, twining, twisting, teeming with insects and squirrels and monkeys and bats.

The horse stopped before one such tree – it was hard to tell if it was one tree or many, there were so many trunks all welded together, rising up high and dense as if it could support heaven itself. At its base, huge roots, some as big as branches, looped out of the earth creating entrances to hollows far beneath. The wild child slid from the horse's back and dived into a hollow, disappearing from sight.

Suddenly Bublu noticed that, not far from the entrance, was a spot which had been scraped out of the earth. It was blackened, and burnt bits of wood were proof of a fire having been lit. His eye roamed round further and alighted upon a metal bowl, darkened by smoke and fire – he almost over-looked it, tucked as it was between the smaller roots of the tree.

'Someone has been living here,' he whispered.

The boys stood hand in hand, wary; alert, ready to run if necessary, yet filled with curiosity.

The sight of the bowl and the pot reminded Sparrow of his empty stomach.

'Bublu, I'm hungry.'

'Yeah, me too. Starving. We could catch the horse and make it take us back through the jungle – but maybe someone lives here; perhaps a holy man. He may help us and tell us what to do, so we'll wait a little to see if Jungli comes out.'

They squatted down on the path, out of the shafts of sunlight, which fell in fiery barbs through any chink in the forest canopy that it could find.

Bublu jerked with surprise. He must have nodded off. He didn't know for how long the wild child had been sitting outside the hollow of the tree gazing at them. Sparrow had toppled over from his squatting position, and lay curled up on the earth, sleeping like a baby.

The older boy got slowly to his feet, his eyes fixed on another figure which was emerging from the hollow – a figure draped in a garment from head to toe. Bublu's heart thudded into his mouth with sudden terror. Who was it? It didn't look like a holy man or any person. Was it a corpse still wrapped in its shroud, somehow come to life? A ghost, or some spirit which had attached itself to the tree? Hunger and fear paralysed his limbs and deadened his brain. He could only watch helplessly, unable to run or hide, while the figure unwound itself from the depths of the earth and finally reached the outside. It rose to its feet and stretched. The garments fell away from the head and shoulders, revealing thin, gaunt arms and long black hair which tumbled out in a great swathe. It was a woman. She turned and, in her face, Bublu saw all the sorrows of the world swimming in her eyes and etched into the lines across her brow and round her mouth.

'I know her,' Bublu murmured.

Rama had gone off to catch the golden deer, but he had made Lakshmana promise that, whatever happened, he would not leave Sita alone. But Rama didn't come back and he didn't come back, and Sita and Lakshmana were filled with anxiety. Suddenly, they heard Rama's voice calling in terror. 'Help me, help me! Lakshmana, come and save me! My life is in danger!'

Lakshmana leapt to his feet and grabbed his bow and arrows. He rushed out of the hut to go his brother's aid. But suddenly he stopped in his tracks, paused and turned back.

'Lakshmana what are you doing?' cried Sita, amazed. 'Why are you not rushing to save your brother?'

'I cannot go, Sita. I promised Rama that I would not leave you alone.'

Then Sita flung herself at him, pushing him towards the forest. 'You must go, you must go, can't you hear him calling for help?'

Rama's voice echoed round the forest, desperately begging, 'Lakshmana, Lakshmana. Help me, brother! My life is in danger.'

Still Lakshmana hesitated. Then, with deadly anger, Sita told him, 'Lakshmana, if you don't go and save Rama, I will never call you brother again; I will never speak to you or be in your presence ever again,' and she looked as if she might, herself, run into the forest to look for her husband.

Lakshmana put out his hand and restrained her gently. He led her back to the hut, then taking an arrow, he drew a circle round the entrance to the hut and said to Sita, 'I have drawn a magic circle round this hut. So long as you stay inside the circle, you will be protected from evil powers. I will go and seek Rama, if you promise me that you will never step outside the circle until we return.'

Sita promised, and Lakshmana fled in search of his brother, leaving her alone.

187

SEVENTEEN

A Twist of Flowers

The harvest season, ending with merriment and festivities, gave way now to the ever-rising, relentless heat. It was as if seven suns burned in the Punjab skies, sucking the land dry, gulping down the rivers and shrivelling the trees till their leaves rattled.

The schoolteacher and his aunt moved their beds up onto the roof as even the nights got so hot that the insides of dwellings became like ovens. The schoolteacher didn't mind. He loved lying under the black sky, working out the glittering constellations and marvelling at the sudden flare of a shooting star. He loved the way the whole commotion of the day died down to the steady nighttime pulse of the croaking frogs and chirruping crickets.

On one such night he awoke. His senses abruptly sharpened to a pinprick. He heard something; or did he just sense it? For as he lay with his eyes wide open staring into the darkness, there was no sound except the crickets and frogs and the distant screech of the nightjar.

Was it Jungli? He was always hoping that the wild child would come back. Aunt still left a vessel of milk and honey out on the verandah. She believed he would return. The teacher got up silently and, taking his torch from under his pillow, leaned over the low parapet which surrounded the roof top. Although the night was spangled with stars, there was only a new crescent moon, which gave very little light. But he didn't want to put on the torch and risk frightening his visitor away. He listened. Was that breathing he could hear? Was that the sound of milk being gulped down and the slightest clink of the copper dish being replaced on the stone step? His eyes strained into the darkness. He was sure someone was there. He finally called out softly, 'Jungli? *Aow bitchu* – come, little child.' There was no sound. At last he flashed on his torch. No one. He went down to the verandah. The milk was gone.

Ever since Jungli had disappeared, the schoolteacher had felt a sense of deep unease and failure. Each evening, he walked in the palace grounds, wandering along the shore of the lake where he had first seen the wild child. Sometimes he felt as though he was being watched, but whether it was by the ghosts of drowned children, or the homeless boys living in the ruins of the palace, he didn't know.

His old aunt was nervous at the thought of him walking there alone. 'It isn't safe. Those boys are getting wilder and more savage – there's no doubt about it.'

Once, he walked to within sight of the palace itself, hoping to catch a glimpse of Nazakhat, who had been one of his pupils, but he was wary. Nazakhat was a Muslim, and there were still plenty of people around ready to kill Muslims. Only the other day, a Muslim family had been caught trying to repossess their old home, sneaking in secretly at night. But they were spotted and the alarm was raised. In no time, armed men – men who had been their neighbours and friends – came brandishing flaming torches and chased them out of town, burning their house to the ground in the process.

There were increasing reports of break-ins and random attacks in their district. People said it was the homeless boys at the palace getting out of control. Their tactics had changed suddenly. Instead of doing odd jobs, or seeking the charity of the villages around, they were operating as a gang, stealing from dwellings and outhouses and terrorising the district.

The clerk's wife was outraged and demanded action. Why, her own sons – her own three, innocent, fat-of-the-land sons – had been attacked while buying *jalaibees* on their way to school. They had run home crying that ragged boys had leapt out of the bushes, kicked them to the ground and snatched the hot treacly sweets from their hands.

The clerk's wife had enfolded all three of her darling boys into her arms and, with a tender thumb, erased the tears from their chubby cheeks and, in a shrill voice, excoriated her husband for not having done something sooner. 'Everybody knows it's those fellows squatting out in the ruined palace. They're worse than jackals. And you just turn a blind eye.'

'Yes, yes, yes . . .' the clerk had intoned wearily. 'I will go and have words with the schoolteacher, Manmohan Singh. He has been thinking about these boys. He wants to try and help them.'

'Help them! Huh!' snorted his wife, unsympathetically. 'The authorities have already made provision. They should be rounded up and sent to the camps and orphanages. Don't go to the schoolmaster with his wishy-washy ideas. Go to the district magistrate, I tell you.'

The clerk sighed. Perhaps she was right. Dutifully, he went all the way into the town to the district magistrate to ask that some action be taken. 'Every day there are reports of break-ins; chickens being stolen, sugar cane cut from the fields and buffaloes milked before they even get home in the evenings. And now they attack my boys. It's got to stop.' The clerk spluttered indignantly and wiped his brow with the end of his dhoti.

But the district magistrate had other more important things on his mind. He showed his boredom by putting his feet up on his desk and filing his nails, till the clerk got the message and crept sheepishly away.

On his way back, the clerk encountered the teacher cycling home from school. Courteously, the teacher dismounted and walked with him for a while. The clerk complained indignantly about the rampaging boys.

'What have you seen of these lads?' he asked. 'Do you recognise any of them? Are they from round here?'

191

'I have glimpsed them,' said the teacher, guardedly. 'Many are from round here – but orphaned or separated from their families. Something must be done, certainly,' agreed the teacher, 'but I would like to rebuild my school again. Most of these boys were born in this district. They have a right to stay, and there is still a chance that surviving relatives will come looking for them in due course. After all, Gandhiji would not have liked us to discriminate against these boys on account of their religion, caste or creed, would he?' He looked slyly sideways at the clerk, who had so rigorously taken up the Gandhian way of life.

'Tch!' The clerk shrugged. 'Gandhiji agreed to this partition.'

'It broke his heart, though,' the teacher reminded him, 'and, more than anything, he believed in a land where all religions could exist side by side.'

'Yes, but he was a practical man and what's done is done. It's no good now, letting sentimentality rule your heart. Besides, the Mahatma is dead. There is no one with the same power that he had. Everything has changed. The Muslims have been driven away from these parts, gone to other villages over the border to their own homeland; and likewise, we now have new families – Hindus and Sikhs who have been kicked out of Pakistan and have been given land and property here. You should not interfere. In any case, I have informed the authorities and I hope these boys will be rounded up soon and taken away.'

'Hmmm.' The teacher stroked his beard thoughtfully. 'That would be a pity. I'd like to take on these boys and educate them. I could turn the palace into a school. Such a building shouldn't go to waste. My own school was burnt to the ground. I need a new one and the palace would be ideal.'

'Well, sir! I think you live in what the Britishers call "cloud-cuckoo-land" but I wish you luck,' and arriving at his house, he saluted the teacher respectfully and went inside.

That evening, instead of going for his usual walk to the lake in the palace grounds, the teacher cycled along the road to the main entrance.

Passing between the broken stone pillars and pillaged iron-wrought gates, almost hidden by banana and pineapple trees grown wild, the teacher cycled cautiously down what had been the main avenue. Huge, widely-spreading mango trees arched over his head and created a dense tunnel, at the far end of which was the palace. As he cycled nearer, he couldn't help marvelling at the massive strength of this building, which neither war nor nature had been able to overcome and, once again, he wished that he could turn it into a centre for learning. Everyone was sick of war and killing. They wanted to rebuild again – and what better place to start with than here? He circled the front of the building with its terraces and balustrades, and dismounted. It would seem better to be on foot if he was noticed, less officious than riding on a bicycle. He hid the bike in undergrowth, and walked instead, trying to look casual.

He left the path and broke across what had once

been spacious, well-watered lawns, to the outer verandahs of the ruined palace. A thin coil of smoke
rose out of the courtyard. He reached the open
courtyard door and peered inside. There they all
were – like a band of brigands. These were the boys
who had caused so much trouble and anger. Yet,
as the teacher could now see, they were nothing
but children. A couple of boys squatted near the
fire, stirring a metal pot which hung from a crudely
made spit. Other clusters of boys milled around,
talking, joking and playing jacks with pieces of
stone. They were engrossed and, at first, didn't see
him. He recognised the boy with the catapult who
had struck the wild child. He was bigger than the
rest, and had the arrogant air of a self-appointed
leader of the pack. He was showing off a penknife
which flashed in his hand while he recounted how
he had stolen it in the bazaar. There was no sign of
Nazakhat.

Then suddenly the teacher was spotted. A quiver
ran through the group. Their heads lifted. They
stared at him, motionless, like a herd of deer, poised
before flight. He held up a hand in a gesture of
peace.

'I am a teacher,' he said boldly. 'Some of you may
know me. I want to help. You know you can't live
like this for ever. Sooner or later, the authorities
will come and round you up. You'll be sent away.
Some of you could go to gaol . . .'

Their faces remained impassive, and the boy they
called 'One Eye' got to his feet and, menacingly,
began fitting a stone to his catapult.

194

The teacher stood his ground. 'Everyone knows you are the ones responsible for all the thefts recently. They're getting fed up. Some might not even bother to wait for the police to do something. Where is your other leader? Has he gone? Is this why you are now behaving like criminals?' He shrugged indifferently at the sight of One Eye's catapult. 'You might bring down a bird or two with that thing, or even a young helpless child,' he said quietly, 'but it won't be much use against the full weight of the law.' Then he appealed to the others. 'It doesn't have to be this way, you know. You have a choice. I am a teacher. I want to teach. I want to start my school again. You can be my pupils, or you can be thugs. Think about it.' Then he deliberately turned his back on them and walked away. He heard the whistle of the stone zipping past his ear and striking the ground in front of him. One Eye hadn't missed – but the Teacher wasn't sure if it was a threat or a challenge. He didn't look back.

Ram Singh was old and bent double with lumbago. Perhaps that's why he survived the massacres which had swept through the area.

First he was abandoned by his nephews and their families, in their mad rush to flee; then even the killers themselves didn't seem to find him worth bothering about. He had sometimes wondered if he was invisible, the way they had ignored him. All around him, people had been hacked to death and their houses burnt, yet time after time he just stood there, trembling with horror or falling down on his knees and begging God for protection, and no one had so much touched a hair of his head.

Because he had lived with his nephews, when their house was destroyed and they had fled, he moved into the church. No one bothered with the church either. Various groups of renegades had swept in, looted it and stripped it bare, but they had at least left the building standing. Unlike the mosque, the temple and gurdwara – which in turn were razed to the ground by their relevant enemies.

All through those bitter winter months, he had lived in the church, sleeping on the pews and using an altar cloth he found for a blanket. Sometimes bands of killers passing through also slept in the church, yet never seemed to see him.

Although Ram Singh had worked for the church for over forty years, being its caretaker and pumping the organ bellows three times a day every Sunday for the Britishers, he was a devout Hindu, and he swore that when the troubles were over, he would go on a pilgrimage to the Ganges – perhaps to Rishikesh – and thank God for his deliverance.

The winter had been hard for him. The worst in all his life. The church was so freezing at night that he had been forced to light a fire in the transept. His lumbago was agonising and, sometimes, he had been locked so rigid in pain that he couldn't even roll off the pew. There were times when he had come close to starvation, because he couldn't get out and about to forage for food.

Of a naturally philosophical disposition, however, Ram Singh comforted himself that being bent double had its advantages. His eyes were permanently fixed downwards to the earth, so he often came upon all sorts of things. He found things which most people would think useless, such as anonymous keys, ripped sandals, an old petrol can or a broken china cup; but he always picked it up and, like an old ant, somehow carried it back to his den and stored it. You never knew nowadays what might suddenly prove to be useful.

It was in this way that he found the treasure of all treasures. Something which was to become his most precious possession; something which made him feel especially blessed by the gods; they had not only preserved his life, but they led him to find the vicar's old wind-up gramophone.

He often shuffled over to the vicarage. It had been looted and ransacked over and over again, so that not one room was intact. How such an item had been overlooked, he could hardly imagine. Perhaps some passing marauder had found it and unable to carry it away, had hidden it, meaning to return. The sun, glinting sharply on something metallic, had drawn Ram Singh's attention to a pile of stones and earth. He had hobbled over slowly, picking his way with difficulty through the rubble. Panting with the exertion, he sat on the pile, and then began to sift his way down to it stone by stone.

After lugging the heavy object back to the church and hiding it behind the altar, he then returned to the vicarage over and over again and systematically hunted through the ruined rooms. Unearthing the gramophone was one thing, but without needles and records, the thing was useless.

It was in a room which had been the vicar's library that he finally found what he was looking for. Thieves and marauders had no use for books, especially those written in English. They contented themselves with knocking down the bookcases and hurling their contents all round the room. Among the scattered books, most of them smashed, trodden into the ground, chipped and cracked, was the vicar's collection of gramophone records.

With a grunt of delight, old Ram Singh went down on his knees and began to extricate them. Any record that had at least one portion of it intact, he set aside. There were performances of Gilbert and Sullivan, arias sung by Gigli, piano sonatas played by Dame Myra Hess and violin pieces performed by Campoli. Ram Singh couldn't read any of the gold-lettered titles, but the labels were pretty, with their different colours and the little dog waiting patiently by the horn of the phonograph. He hunted a further hour, looking for needles, but in vain. When, finally, he hobbled back to the church, clutching an armful of records, he found that a packet of needles had been tucked away inside the gramophone all along.

Red is an auspicious colour, and anyway it was his favourite colour, so he selected a record with a red label. He placed it on the turntable, fitted a needle and turned the handle to wind it up. With a somewhat shaky hand, he guided the arm across the record to an unchipped part and set it down.

Ram Singh almost straightened out with shocked pleasure, as the piercingly sweet sound of a violin echoed up to the rafters. 'Ah ha ha . . .' Ram Singh patted his heart with ecstasy and shook his head with critical admiration. He recalled the old days when, each evening, such a sound would issue from the Chadwicks' bungalow.

Someone moved through the long grass, weaving in and out of the almost hidden grave-stones, making no sound louder than a thin summer wind riffling through the brown dry stalks. The person paused briefly outside the west door, listening to the violin, then continued down to the far end of the cemetery, to the grave of the Chadwick twins, lying in the shade under a temple tree. Deft fingers laid a twist of fresh flowers on top of the slab of grey stone, then swiftly left.

Later, when Ram Singh went on his usual evening patrol among the graves, which he tended as best he could, he was startled to come across the little garland. He couldn't help a shiver. No one but he ever came to the cemetery. No one but he had tended the grave of the Chadwick twins since the departure of the family two years back. Had the violin summoned some ghost from the past? He set aside the record with the red label and, for a long time, only played the records with the yellow or blue labels, so as not to invoke the ghost again. Not that he was afraid. A man of his age knew no fear – not even of ghosts. But he was not yet ready to confront the past.

However, some days later, when the garland had withered on the tomb, another twist of fresh flowers appeared in its place.

EIGHTEEN

A Boat on a Pond

'What's it like, Jaspal, living with poshies?' Billy asked the question with a look on his face which suggested a distasteful answer.

Jaspal stared gloomily into the dark waters of the pond. The dhow his father had made him rested on the grass verge. It had not yet had its maiden voyage. Now that it lay next to the yacht Billy's father had made, it looked crude and amateurish. You could see where a tool had hacked and chipped away at the shape of the body, and hollowed out the open belly.

'Did you make it yourself?' was Billy's first remark on seeing the dhow, and Jaspal had nodded a yes. He was too ashamed to say his father had made it. Billy's boat could have been bought in a shop – it was so smooth and sleek and brightly painted with that special glossy yacht paint, which gleamed in the sunlight. The dhow was just raw wood and its curved mast looked more like the rough branch of a tree, whereas Billy's had a tall straight mast with three yard-arms, and rigging as fine as a spider's web.

Jaspal had skipped afternoon school in Richmond and, instead, clutching his dhow, had taken the underground to Clapham and waited outside Billy's house for him to come home from school.

Jaspal had been intensely pleased by his boat – until he saw Billy's, then he felt annoyed and humiliated.

'What's it like living with snobs?' Billy asked him again. It was the first time they had met since Jaspal had been so abruptly moved to Richmond.

What's it like . . . what's it like? Stupid words. Stupid question. How could he answer? Jaspal was full of rages which he didn't understand. He felt he was being kicked around to suit other people – and there was no one he could trust. He hated his father for being what he was. His mother? He refused to think about her. She was dead. He couldn't even see her face in his mind. He used to try – and every time, there was just a blank. So he was convinced she was dead.

There was only Marvinder. She had never stopped loving him. She was the only person in the world . . . yes . . . he mustn't forget Marvinder. He could trust her – except – she wasn't angry as he was. She was sad; she was hurting inside. He sometimes found her crying. But she never blamed anyone, and wouldn't say a word against their father. He wished just once, she would yell and scream and be nasty. As nasty as he could be. Most of the time he wanted to kick something, punch something, kill something. He clenched his fists and thought, when I grow up . . . when I grow up . . . I'll . . .'

'Is it very grand? Tons better than Whitworth

Road, eh? I mean – you live in a house, don't yer?' Billy sounded envious.

'Yeah. It's all right,' muttered Jaspal. 'At least I get a room to myself. That's better than sharing with Patrick and Michael – coming in at all hours, stinking of beer and cigarettes – and snoring all night.'

'Well, that's something, I suppose,' commented Billy.

'But I hate the school.' Jaspal said this with such ferocity that Billy stared in silence, unsure what to say.

'I could kill them all, especially that headmaster.' Jaspal remembered the interview when Mr Chadwick had accompanied him on that first day.

'Jaspal's a bright lad,' Mr Chadwick had told Mr Borden, the headmaster. 'English is his second language. He couldn't read it when he arrived. But he has caught up remarkably well, and is particularly good at arithmetic.'

'Hmmm . . .' Mr Borden looked sceptical. A telephone call to Jaspal's old school had already alerted him to the fact that Jaspal often played truant and got into fights. No one at his Clapham school had spoken of him as being good at anything. In fact, they thought he was a perfect nuisance.

'Well, I hope he'll behave himself, that's all. I pride myself on a disciplined school.' Mr Borden couldn't disguise the distaste he felt for this boy. 'Could he be prevailed upon not to wear that thing?' He referred disparagingly to the turban.

'I must wear my turban.' Jaspal almost spat out the words. 'It is my religion.'

'Yes,' agreed Mr Chadwick, supportively. 'Jaspal is a Sikh. He must wear his turban.'

'Pity. He's sure to come in for some ragging then,' said the headmaster with a sigh.

'Jaspal is pretty good at taking care of himself,' Mr Chadwick assured him.

'Well, I just hope it doesn't lead to fighting. I do not like fighting in my school. Anyone caught fighting — anywhere — inside or out in the playground, gets the cane. Do you understand?' Mr Borden spoke slowly and loudly, as if Jaspal were deaf and half-witted.

Jaspal nodded. There was something faintly impudent in the nod. Mr Borden made a mental note. Dumb insolence, he thought to himself, and looked forward to breaking his spirit.

'Of course, Jaspal's class is in preparation for the eleven-plus. I don't expect he has much of a chance, but we can't treat him differently from the rest. He'll just have to muck in.'

'He'll do what he can,' said Mr Chadwick.

So for the second time in England, Jaspal walked into a classroom, and a whole sea of faces seem to turn in one movement and stare at him. For the second time, they sniggered at his turban, mispronounced his name and rapidly reeled off the abuse with which he had become familiar. As an added insult, however, the Richmond children called him Jap. It seemed logical to them as the Japanese had been a wartime enemy, and the children had decided that Jaspal should be an enemy. So Jap seemed a perfectly appropriate name to call him.

No one in his last school had cared much about the eleven-plus, so Jaspal hadn't either. The exam would decide whether he went to a grammar school or to a secondary modern. As none of his friends had expected to go to the grammar school, neither had Jaspal. They said it was for posh children and swots. Already the battle lines were being drawn up and the abuse rehearsed; those at the secondary moderns would jeer at the grammar-school pupils and call them 'Sissies', and the grammar-school children would respond with shouts of 'Blockheads!' And that was the least of the trouble. Given half a chance, both sides would beat each other up, such was the bitterness of the divide.

In any case, whatever school they went to, staying on at school after fifteen was unthinkable to most of Jaspal's friends; not even to be considered. 'What's the point?' they argued. 'Better to go out and get a job. Start earning.' There were plenty of factories all round Clapham, and just downriver were the docks. It wasn't hard to find a job starting at seven and sixpence a week and, for many poor families, the sooner an extra wage came in, the better. So at his old school in Clapham, hardly anyone expected or wanted to go to grammar school, let alone on to university.

But Richmond was different. Parents were so keen for their children to pass the eleven-plus, they even bribed them with promises of luxuries, such as bicycles or train sets or money.

It was all right for Marvinder, she was too old for the eleven-plus. She just went to the local secondary modern and missed all the fuss.

'What sort of boat is that, then?' asked Billy, referring to the dhow and trying to keep the ridicule out of his voice.

Jaspal replied haughtily. He wouldn't show the discomfort he felt about his boat being so rough. 'It's the sort of boat you see all round the Indian Ocean. They can even sail to Africa.'

'Liar!' chirped Billy good-humouredly. 'I bet it couldn't even sail across this pond. Come on, let's get the boats in the water. I'll race you.' Billy jumped to his feet, picked up his shining yacht and went to the water's edge. 'My dad copied one of those old clipper ships that used to sail to America. Look, he painted its name on the side.'

Jaspal looked, begrudgingly at the fine brush-work near the prow. *Princess Rose.*

'After Princess Margaret. Her second name is Rose,' explained Billy.

Jaspal took his dhow and placed it in the water next to Billy's boat. 'I haven't got round to painting mine yet. I wanted to see if it would float first,' muttered Jaspal, desperately hoping that his boat would at least stay upright in the water.

Billy licked a finger and held it up in the air. 'The wind's coming from this way, so we can sail the boats from here to the other side.' He pointed across the width of the pond which was about six metres.

The boys angled their prows and adjusted their sails. At least, Billy made a great thing of fiddling with the rigging, while Jaspal simply unfurled the one piece of cloth which acted as a sail and tied it down to the stern of his boat. It flapped slightly, and the surface of the pond shivered and wrinkled. Jaspal felt a sudden thrill. He tossed up a silent prayer. 'Please, God, let my boat sail.'

They each held the stern and Billy called out, 'Ready . . . steady . . . go!' Each gave his boat a firm shove and sent in out across the water.

For a while, the two vessels moved forward with the thrust and sailed out a metre from the shore. The boys hopped up and down excitedly, cheering on their own. Then the boats hesitated and slowed down as the wind dropped.

At this stage, Billy's boat was in front. It looked a perfect picture of a boat, its blue and white painted body reflecting proudly in the water and its sails taut and arched in the breeze. It was like a beautiful bird, which any minute might fly.

In contrast, Jaspal's dhow looked heavy and clumsy. There was nothing elegant about it, it was more like a lump of wood than a boat, and its sail looked just like the scrap of canvas that it was. A boat with no name – just as well, thought Jaspal, for if Billy's boat was as beautiful as a swan, Jaspal's was certainly an ugly duckling. Yet, briefly, his bit of canvas had caught the wind and billowed promisingly.

The boys stared helplessly at their boats, becalmed in the still flat water, just out of reach.

'Mine's in front,' declared Billy. 'I'm winning.'

'Only a little,' retorted Jaspal. 'We're neck and neck, if you ask me.'

They got sticks and churned up the water in an effort to get some movement. 'Oh where's that wind. Come on, wind!' the boys shouted.

Obediently, the wind gusted up again. Harder this time. It ruffled the feathers of the ducks who were preening themselves on the island in the middle. It rustled the reeds growing out from the banks. It sent spirals of ripples juddering across the water. The boats rocked. The wind caught their sails. They quivered. Then the bit of canvas that was Jaspal's sail suddenly billowed out, and the dhow shot forward at great speed.

'Hey! Look at mine!' yelled Jaspal, leaping about with glee. But he was stopped short by a wail of anguish from Billy, as the same wind seemed to slap at his yacht and, without any warning, tipped it over on its side.

The boys gazed in horror, as the beautiful mast, its white sails and delicate rigging sank beneath the green surface of the pond.

A disabled war veteran, watching from his wheel-chair, thrust the wheels round with his hands and rolled over to them. 'Reckon your mast was too tall for the boat, laddie,' he said to Billy, sympathetically. 'Unbalanced it, that's all. It can be fixed. But by golly, look at that one.' He gazed in admiration at the dhow which had almost reached the other side. 'I used to see them things when we was round the Gulf during the war. Incredible boats.

208

The design hasn't changed in three thousand years, and you can see why.'

While Jaspal raced round to the other side of the pond to retrieve his dhow before it crashed into the bank, Billy was disconsolately pulling off his shoes and socks and rolling up his trousers.

'What's the time, please, mister?' Jaspal asked the war veteran, who for a while held the victorious dhow on his lap and ran his fingers admiringly over its hewn body.

'Six-thirtyish,' he replied glancing at his watch.

'Oi! Billy! I'm off!' yelled Jaspal to his friend, who was knee-high in the middle of the pond, trying to retrieve his unfortunate yacht.

'Will you be at the gang meeting after school, Friday?' cried Billy.

'Of course!' Jaspal was still the leader, even if he had moved away.

'I used to see these things, sailing round the Gulf and in the Indian Ocean,' murmured the war veteran, reluctantly handing Jaspal back his boat. 'Did you say your dad made it? He's a clever fellow then. Got it just right.'

Jaspal grinned, then set off running – and as he ran, he chanted Hanuman ... Hanuman ... for he felt as though he would fly like the wind.

Where there is night, there is day; where there is light, there is darkness; where there is good, there is evil. That's the way Lord Brahma made things. God creates and destroys – as though in order to have one, you must have the other. When Lord

Brahma instructed Manu to build an ark and save the seed of every living thing from the flood, he told Manu that he must not just store the seed of the angels in the heavens, but also the demons in the bowels of the earth, who were to await the time when he would create the world all over again. But sometimes it's hard to tell demons from angels.

One Eye stood on the top terrace of the palace and looked at all the land that lay around him. He was like Ravana, king of the demons. He could almost believe that he was the ruler of all that he surveyed. No one was stronger than he; he felt invincible; there was no Rama to kill him.

He watched the boys far below him milling around in the courtyard – and smiled. They were now in his power and would do anything that he asked them. He had told them that Bublu was their enemy, that because he was a Muslim, he would have betrayed them all one day. Now Bublu had gone. It had been so simple. No fight, no blood. All he had had to do was sow the seed of doubt in their minds, and their trust turned to suspicion. Bublu, who they thought was their friend, was suddenly their enemy.

A feeling of power surged through One Eye. He breathed deeply and expanded his chest and flexed his muscles. He almost felt that if he threw himself from the terrace he would fly. He climbed on top of the parapet.

'Aiyeee! Aiyee!' he shouted at the top of his voice.

The boys stared up in horror, gathering themselves together in a tight huddle. Already they feared him. He spoke the language of violence and bullying; he was organising them to rob and steal. They had become a band of thugs.

Suddenly One Eye saw the white horse. He didn't know how it had come or why it was there. It was as if it had been sent just for him, for there it was, standing right beneath him, waiting to be mounted; and a voice in his head seemed to whisper, 'If you are the ruler of all rulers, then you should have a horse.'

'Yes, yes! The horse is for me!' Wildly, he turned and raced down the stone steps, down and down till he reached the ground, then he ran all the way round to where the horse was still standing.

He stopped at the corner of the terrace, containing his excitement and his desire to take over the animal.

The horse raised its head, aware of his presence. One Eye began to walk slowly forward, his arm outstretched, his fingers taut, ready to grasp the loose reins. Nearer, nearer. He could hear the breath in its nostrils, he could smell the sweat on its flanks. Nearer he walked; his fingers almost touched the reins, when suddenly the horse turned its head and One Eye found himself looking into the eye of the horse. The eye seemed to grow bigger and bigger and One Eye felt as though he was being sucked into its depths. It was like the third eye of Shiva. Its gaze seemed to pierce him like a sword; it rooted him to the ground; it struck him dumb. Now he seemed to be swirling round and round as if caught in a vortex which would eventually suck him down

211

into the very centre of the universe. Desperately, he reached out for the reins. The horse reared up; its great body blotted out the sky and then a multitude of hooves came thundering down upon his head.

NINETEEN

'La Paloma'

Marvinder continued her music. It mattered less and less where she was. She went back to Clapham from time to time to play to Dr Silbermann but, though he was always pleased to see her, somehow it wasn't the same. He seemed older suddenly, and she would catch his attention drifting, and his face moulding into sadness. One day Dr Sildermann said, 'Play, my dear, play that bit of Bach. I don't want to teach you today, I just want to listen,' and he sat back in his armchair, his body crumpling, oblivious of all the music and papers which he crushed beneath him.

She played. It seemed important to play her best. Her fingers vibrated powerfully on the strings, and she drew her bow up and down, easing out the melody. As she played, she remembered how she and Patrick had sat on the back stairs together, secretly listening to Dr Silbermann. His playing had somehow brought them together and, now – if only ... if only ... she imagined that somehow Patrick would be drawn again to the back stairs and was maybe, even now, sitting out there, listening to her and remembering that Truth and Beauty were the most important things in the world.

When she came to the end, she held her bow suspended in the air, while the sound died away, and she suddenly realised that Dr Silbermann hadn't moved. Silently, she brought her arm down and laid her violin back in its case. Was he asleep? He didn't seem to be breathing. His thin, bony wrists drooped motionless over the arms of the chair, and though his head was tilted back, his jaw hung slack like one asleep – or – like one who is dead?

'Dr Silbermann?' Her voice broke out, panic-stricken.

His eyes flew open.

'Oh . . .' Marvinder laughed with relief. 'I thought you were . . . I thought you had gone to sleep.'

'My body was here in this room – an empty shell. Your playing took my spirit, dear child, and carried it far, far away. For a while I played with my daughters and talked with my wife. It is a terrible thing if one only remembers their last expressions – those expressions of hideous terror as the Nazis wrenched us apart from each other. I think you understand. You helped me to remember their laughter; remember the days when we were happy. Thank you. Thank you.' The tears streamed down his face as he leant back once more and closed his eyes, and Marvinder knew that she could do no more, but leave him to his grief.

The festival hardly mattered now. Not the festival. What mattered more and more was that she played and, now she lived in a house where music was the common language, she knew that she could play as much as she liked and no one would complain. When the day of the festival drew closer, her only concern was that she play well enough to win her section, so that she would definitely perform at the winners' concert. But it was not the winning that mattered. Only that Patrick had promised to come.

She hardly noticed the nervous prattle of parents and children as they milled around in the large echoing hall, where the preliminary stages were held. One by one, girls and boys went solemnly up onto the platform, followed by earnest accompanists, who sat at the piano and peered over the tops of the music, waiting for the signal to begin. She didn't sit with a critical ear, listening to the shaky fingers sliding out of tune, or the wobbly bows which screeched with fright; nor did she feel jealousy or concern when someone played well, and the hall burst into approving applause. She just waited quietly, with head down and hands clasped calmly in her lap. Harold Chadwick admired her poise. He gave his wife, Dora, a confident nod when at last their turn came, and she followed Marvinder up onto the platform.

'La Paloma.' The lilting accompaniment filled the hall and transformed it from the brown, dusty interior of the local church hall, to the blue waves of the Mediterranean, rippling up against the sides of the bobbing fishing boat. It was a simple enough composition, requiring no great skill or technique, but Marvinder played it dreamily, yearningly and was able, briefly, to halt the shuffling and fidgeting which rumbled in the background.

When she returned to her seat, her face flushed with the enthusiastic applause which exploded after her performance, Harold Chadwick patted her quietly saying, 'That was good, Marvi. That was very good.'

Then they had to wait for the result. Marvinder sat totally still. She never looked up, even when the adjudicator began going through all the competitors, giving each one a little critical appreciation and then announcing their mark. The Chadwicks thought she was being composed and mature, they didn't realise the torment that raged inside her, that her fists were clenched at her sides, and that she had called on all the powers that be in the universe, to let her win.

She heard her name. She heard the praise; how good her intonation was; her bowing and vibrato and, most of all, the feeling with which she played. 'I award Marvinder Singh the highest mark of the section, ninety per cent,' the adjudicator said. There was a gasp, and everyone looked round and then burst into applause.

'It's amazing that you seem to understand our music so well,' commented the kindly adjudicator, when she went up to get her certificate.

'Thank you,' murmured Marvinder, wondering what on earth she meant by 'our music'.

'I look forward to you playing at the winners' concert.'

It was to be a glorious day – a victorious day. She had planned for it for so long. She would play at the winners' concert – and Patrick would be there, and she would play so beautifully that he would be spellbound, and would never again make jokes about her caterwauling. And she had an image of herself in her mind's eyes – not dressed in her satin pink Punjabi tunic and pyjamas, which Mrs Chadwick had recommended, but wearing a party dress Edith said she could borrow – a green softly flowing dress, with a V-neck and no sleeves. She wouldn't wear her hair in schoolgirl plaits, but undo it and have it flowing long and loose down her back. She wanted to look like one of those film stars, so that when Patrick saw her, he'd gasp admiringly, 'Hey! Take a look at Marvi!'

She told Mrs Chadwick that she would go to Clapham straight after school one day during the following week, so that she could tell the O'Gradys and Dr Silbermann that she was playing in the concert.

She went first to the O'Gradys', bounding up the front steps and, finding the front door open as usual, thudding up further to the first floor, yelling out for Kathleen and Mrs O'Grady. It felt like being home, for no matter how nice the house was in Richmond; no matter how luxurious it was to walk on soft carpets and to sleep in a beautiful white-sheeted bed all on her own, she had learned to love the O'Gradys for their rough kindness and the way in which they had absorbed her and Jaspal into the home, as if they had belonged all along. And despite everything – even Mr O'Grady who never seemed to like them or their father – she felt full of affection for that large, noisy family.

With her face laughing and flushed, she knocked on the door to the O'Grady flat, pushing it open as she did so. 'Hello! Kath . . .' She stopped short and the smile fell from her face.

'Why, Marvi!' Patrick disentangled himself from the sofa and a girl, whose arms had been draped around him. He stood up sheepishly, pushing back his brown, curly hair and straightening his pullover. 'Hey, fancy seeing you here!' He looked embarrassed.

'I . . . I'm sorry,' stammered Marvinder. 'I thought Kathy or Mammy would be home. I just wanted to tell them that I would be playing at the festival winners' concert next Saturday. I . . . I thought . . . maybe . . . Kathy might come and see me . . . sorry, Patrick!' and she turned and fled back down the stairs.

'Hey, Marvi!' Patrick choked awkwardly. He ran to the landing and shouted over the banister. 'Marvi, wait!' But she left without looking back, slamming the front door behind her.

'Who was that girl, Paddy?' drawled a languid voice. A pretty young woman took out a comb from her blonde hair and swept her tresses up into it once more, before uncrossing her nyloned legs and raising a hand to the young man, for help to rise from the sofa. 'Was she one of them blackies belonging to Govind?'

Patrick ignored the outstretched hand. 'Oh shut

it, Irene,' he muttered. 'Her name's Marvinder – get it?' and, feeling unreasonably angry, he moved over to the mantelpiece and lit up a cigarette.

'Oh, pardon me, I'm sure. Didn't expect you to be sensitive about a schoolgirl – let alone a darky.' She studied him mockingly, then got herself to her feet. She glanced at her watch. 'If we leave now, we'd be in time for the start of that Stewart Grainger film on at the Palladium. Do you still fancy it?' She tipped her head coyly on one side.

'Yeah, sure. Let's go.' He took a coat off the door and held it for her while she put it on.

She turned and kissed him hard on the lips. He hardly responded. She gripped his chin between her fingers and forced him to meet her gaze. 'Hey, lover boy! You can do better than that, eh?' and she kept her mouth upturned towards him. His eyes slid away from hers, but obediently he kissed her hard on the lips; then, slinging his jacket over his shoulder, took her elbow and, almost fiercely, guided her out of the flat.

Marvinder had dashed down into the basement and let herself noiselessly into Dr Silbermann's darkened hallway, where she buried herself among his jackets and coats which hung in a clump on the pegs. She was gasping with emotion and tears boiled over, scalding her red cheeks. That was Irene. The Irene he danced with at the Palais. Why had she forgotten Irene? Kathy had told her how he danced with Irene – that they were like Fred Astaire and Ginger Rogers! 'They walk out together,' Kathy had told her. So how could she have forgotten

Irene? She felt such a fool. Irene was a grown-up – a lady, not a schoolgirl. She looked like a film star all the time – of course Patrick would love her. Of course he wouldn't even dream of loving Marvinder. Of course not!

She clutched a jacket to her and sobbed bitterly.

'Who's there?' Dr Silbermann had come out of his room. He heard the snuffling among the coats and boots, he saw her ankles sticking out and her clenched knuckles. He gently pulled aside the jacket and raincoat and revealed Marvinder's stricken face.

'Eei yi yi yi!' He sighed, pulling her towards him and hugging her. 'My poor child. What has happened? Never mind, dear. It was your first time. Hardly anyone wins first time round. You can try again next year.' He spoke to her soothingly, while she burst into fresh tears and was unable to explain why she was crying.

He got her a drink of tea and pulled out his paper bag of broken biscuits. At last, her shoulders stopped heaving and her breathing steadied. She sipped the tea and allowed the hot liquid to trickle down her throat and send a glow through her insides. At last she looked up at his kindly face.

'I came first, Doctor,' she said simply. 'I got ninety per cent. Will you come next Saturday night and watch me play in the concert?'

Dr Silbermann seemed to positively swell with pride. 'You won? You won? Oh yipeee!' He pulled her to her feet and whirled her round the room in a Viennese waltz while he sang out 'The Blue

220

Danube' at the top of his voice. 'You're a genius!' he cried. 'My prize pupil,' and he kissed her loudly on both cheeks.

On her way home, she huddled into a corner of the bus. Life hardly seemed worth living now. She wouldn't have cared if she broke her arm, or if something happened to stop her playing. Only one thought made her feel a little better – if only in a bitter way – 'One thing he'll never learn from Irene,' Marvinder whispered out loud with a sense of triumph. 'He'll never learn about Truth and Beauty from her.'

It was a large echoing Victorian hall, with tall arched windows and ornate alcoves. The platform was huge and high, with one shining black grand piano dominating the space.

Marvinder had arrived early for a rehearsal, and took fright. Her stomach seemed to tip upside down and her hands perspired so much she though the violin would slip out of her grip. She wanted to be a million miles away, and wondered how she could have ever wanted to play at the concert. She was glad Dora Chadwick was with her as her accompanist.

Mrs Chadwick talked to her gently as they watched the children up one by one and rehearse their piece. 'Don't forget,' whispered Mrs Chadwick. 'This evening, you are giving a performance, not taking a test or an exam. You will have an audience out there who will not just hear you, but they will see you, too. So you must walk on calmly and nicely – you first, followed by me. They will clap; you will give them a little bow to acknowledge their clapping; and then you and I will look at each other, waiting for everyone to settle down. When the hall is totally quiet, you will give me a little nod to begin and I will play the introduction. When you have finished playing, you will step forward and bow low. I will give a little bow from the piano. Then you will walk off the platform, followed by me.'

After the rehearsal, there was time to go home again, have tea and dress. Marvinder felt too sick to eat. She put on the flowing green dress, and brushed out her hair so that it fell in great ripples down to her waist. She stared at herself in Mrs Chadwick's long mirror, turning sideways, this way then that. She examined herself for a long time in minute detail, then gave a deep sigh. This was the image she wanted. This is how she hoped Patrick would have seen her.

The waiting was the worst part. Marvinder wasn't to play until just before the interval. Before her were at least nine children. Mrs Chadwick was wrong when she said this wasn't a test. For Marvinder, this was a huge test – a test to see if she could overcome bitter disappointment and jealousy; not let herself down because of someone else, but just play as well as she knew she could play. They all wished her luck – Harold Chadwick, Edith and Jaspal. They would be there with their fingers crossed for her, they assured her. She and Dora

Chadwick went on ahead. They would wait back-stage in the green room.

Marvinder was aware of the vast empty hall spreading out below the platform. Excited children kept peeping out through the curtains and exclaiming, 'It's filling up!' Others were squeaking, 'There's Granny! There's Uncle George and Connie and Jack,' and so there was a continuous commentary describing the proceedings as the audience poured in and the clock ticked closer to the starting time.

Suddenly, they were off. On went the first – a brave boy who sat down at the piano and played very loudly and very fast. It gave them courage and, with the audience clapping for all they were worth, the next went on and then the next and the next. It was going well. The children emerged from the platform beaming with joy and relief and glowing with pride at all the fuss and applause. Marvinder waited. Her face was solemn. Dora Chadwick felt a tremor of anxiety. Marvinder had seemed so thrilled to win her place at the winners' concert, now, instead of looking excited she looked hard-faced; uninterested – almost like a zombie. She had tried to share her mood; reassure her if she was nervous, but Marvinder was withdrawn, like a sleepwalker.

'It's our turn, dear,' she murmured, touching her arm. Marvinder turned and looked at her, yet didn't seem to see. However, she nodded, picked up her violin and went into the wings of the platform. An organiser held them back until the applause for the previous performer had died away, then he whispered, 'Good luck,' and ushered them on.

It was Dora who felt afraid. The long walk across the stage seemed endless. Marvinder went first. She seemed to glide, the green dress billowing slightly as she went to the very centre front of the stage. While she waited for Dora to settle herself with the music. Marvinder's eyes wandered out over the sea of upturned faces before her. Then, suddenly, her heart somersaulted. There was a sailor in the audience, far far away at the back. He looked smart and new, in his naval uniform with its shining white stripe and with his curly hair closely clipped to a short back and sides. 'Patrick?' She breathed a silent question. 'Patrick? Is it Patrick?' The lights were so dim; he was so distant – and yet his eyes seemed to gleam, mockingly . . . she looked and looked. Then she heard a little cough. She turned to see Dora gazing intently, her face filled with anxiety, wondering when Marvinder would look at her and give her the signal to play. To her amazement, Marvinder not only turned towards her swiftly, but her face had suddenly come alive and was radiant with smiles. Dora beamed back joyfully, nodded and began to play the introductory chords.

Maybe that was Patrick at the back, maybe it wasn't. It didn't matter. She was playing to Patrick wherever he was. Marvinder's bow came down on the strings so powerfully and rhythmically, that many couldn't help rocking in time to the music. She played her best. Better than her best. She played boldly and freely, as if she really believed that this was Truth and Beauty and that one day she would go and play like that in Barcelona, just to show those silly boys, Patrick and Michael!

She finished to a shout of 'Bravo' and there was such a roar of enthusiasm from the floor that it sounded to Marvinder as if she stood under a waterfall. She bowed, as Dora had taught her and, as she bowed, her eyes again roamed over all the faces below her. She saw Edith and Jaspal; she saw Kathleen and Mrs O'Grady and dear Dr Silbermann, who blew her kisses from outstretched arms; but her eyes swept frantically on, further back, looking for the sailor, but she couldn't find him.

Then she saw Harold Chadwick. He hadn't been sitting with Edith and Jaspal. He was standing near the door, and someone was with him. Someone dark; looking uneasy and awkward; someone alien to her, yet deeply familiar. Marvinder turned and almost ran from the stage.

'Marvinder!' Dora followed her, and clasped her with joy. 'Dearest, you were wonderful. A true musician. Your mother would be so proud.'

'And my father?' cried Marvinder.

Govind was free.

The sight of her father created an earthquake in Marvinder's heart. She didn't know where to find stable ground. She wanted to stay, yet she wanted to flee. She wanted to laugh, yet she wanted to cry. She wanted to find her mother more than anything, yet she was afraid. What if her mother was dead? Jaspal thought she was. Now that her father was free, Marvinder wanted to rejoice. Now they could go back to India; but then she wanted to run out into the night seeking Patrick, beseeching him to take her with him; for if her mother was alive, then how could she bear the pain of finding her, only to be wrenched apart once more because her marriage would be arranged and they would be separated again?

How often had she remembered Patrick's words; gone over those moments in her mind, when they had sat on the stairs together and he had asked in a puzzled voice, 'You wouldn't want to marry a stranger, would you, Marvi?'

If she had known then that the one short time she and Patrick had been together, listening to Dr Silbermann playing the violin, would glimmer for ever like a pale jewel in her heart, she would have paid more attention, made him sit longer, with his bony knees sticking into her back.

Suddenly Kathleen was at her side. She looked shy – even awestruck. She held out a single rose. 'Patrick asked me to give you this. There's a note with it.'

Marvinder tried to stop her heart somersaulting out of her chest. Kathleen threw her arms round her. 'Oh, Marvi! You were wonderful!'

He had scribbled on the back of an envelope.

Dear Marvi,
    I came – just as I promised. I'm sorry I couldn't stay to speak to you in person and say goodbye. I have to catch the train tonight for Plymouth where I'm joining a ship. Marvi,

guess what? I may get to India before you do. We're going out to Burma, and we'll stop at Bombay on the way. I wish you were going to be there. Then you could show me round.

But Marvi, I just wanted to tell you this. You remember you said you would show me Truth and Beauty if I came to hear you play? Well, you did. You played like an angel and I'll never call it caterwauling again.

Me mam says your dad is out of prison now. I guess that means you're going home at last. Perhaps we'll bump into each other again somewhere across the world, eh? Or we'll wave to each other from the decks as our ships pass on the ocean. God bless you, Marvi.

All my love, Patrick.

P.S. Did anyone ever tell you that you look like Ava Gardner – especially when you let your hair loose like that?

Marvinder looked up, her eyes full and her heart heaving. Faces surrounded her, so excited and friendly; faces she loved – but not Patrick's. How could he be here – only to be gone? She saw Mrs O'Grady, standing awkwardly in a corner watching her. She had put on her best coat and hat to come and, as they looked at each other, she had a feeling that Mrs O'Grady knew.

'Well, that was a fine thing to be sure,' murmured Mrs O'Grady, giving her a rough kiss. She had never been one for physical demonstrations of affection. 'It's a pity Mr O'Grady couldn't have heard you, he might have forgiven you for all the practising you used to do.'

Marvinder wanted to hang on to Mrs O'Grady and Kathleen. But they were moving now towards the door. 'Come and see us, Marvinder. Let us know what's going to happen to you. Tell us if you go back to India, won't you.'

'Oh yes, Mammy! I will. I'll come and see you soon.'

Then Dr Silbermann came and, as if she were a princess took up her hand, bowed very low and kissed it. 'You made me very proud tonight, my child,' he said with emotion. 'Thank you. Thank you. You played like a true artist.' He kissed her hand again, then turned quickly and left.

'I'll come and see you soon, Doctor,' Marvi called after him.

At last, she turned to meet her father.

TWENTY

Monsoon

And so the world turned like a great chariot wheel. Each day, the mighty sun god, Surya, undisputed ruler of the heavens, galloped across the skies, his seven horses pulling him in fiery splendour.

All through the hot season, the farmers laboured and sweated, their eyes to the ground, as they reaped their harvest. But there would be no respite yet; no sooner were the crops lifted from the earth, than the farmers, rewrapping their turbans against the force of the sun, attached their bullocks and camels to the plough.

Relentlessly, the soil is turned, furrowed and seeded once more, before the land bakes as hard as iron and the rivers run dry.

Still the heat grows and would be unbearable, if every man, woman and child did not know Nature's calendar. Oh, Surya, you may rule supreme, but praise be to Lord Indra, the thunder god and bringer of rain. Each day now, eyes glance up into the burning blue . . . watching . . . waiting. Deliverance will come; the world will not succumb to the drought demons and be swallowed up in fire.

Each dawn and sunset, the teacher stands on his roof. These are the only times of day that are bearable now. He will bathe and say his prayers and contemplate the universe. Then, after eating breakfast with his aunt, he will cycle down the long white road to school.

The day always comes – it will be the end, if it doesn't – the day always comes, when that first dark smudge appears in the sky. It wanders, like a maiden without a partner, shyly, disconcerted, feeling self-conscious; but not far behind, is another and another. Clouds come ambling along, fat and grey and huge as elephants. Maiden-shy gives way to rampaging boisterousness, as the winds blow up, swirling the dust into the faces of man and beast.

It is time! It is time! The sky darkens; the clouds swell to breaking point – and then one drop of liquid plummets to earth and splatters the dust. A great cry is heard all over the land – so loud and joyful, the gods must hear it from their palaces in the Himalayas and smile. At last, with a thunderous blow from his trident, Indra releases the rain. The children in their classrooms, the clerks in their offices, the businessmen in their leather chairs, the shopkeepers crouched on their cushions – they all tumble out laughing and squealing and singing for joy; umbrellas which have been open against the heat of the sun are folded away. With arms outstretched and mouths up-turned, they swallow and bathe and drench themselves in the monsoon rains; and the farmers, who can do no more, withdraw to the tea houses.

The monsoon came to the forest too. The wind and

rain stirred the dry, brown undergrowth, making it sizzle and squeal. It drew out the animals and insects and reptiles, and the parrots exploded into the air with ecstatic shrieks. It swelled the half-dead river.

Bublu and Sparrow had made themselves a dwelling, half inside the hollow of a great tree. They collected the largest, broadest leaves they could find to carpet the bare earth and they combined the leaves with branches to create a roof and walls. They made their shelter just in time before the rains came.

They had chosen a spot not too close to the woman's tree, but near enough. Bublu said, 'We will watch her and do as she does; eat what she eats, and then we will survive as she has.'

The woman never acknowledged them, even though they used the same river to bathe and drink and often followed her along the forest tracks in search of herbs and fruit and wild berries. But neither did she shy away. It was almost as if she had been expecting them. They knew each other, Bublu was sure of that – and one day, when it was safe to do so, they would speak again as friends and neighbours.

The wild child and the horse seemed to come and go freely – but when they came it was always to her. When they went, Bublu wondered if it was always back to the village.

One day, when there was a break in the rain, the woman emerged from her hollow beneath the peepul tree. She was wrapped in a shawl, and carried a large banana leaf in case it should rain. Bublu noticed that she also carried a freshly woven garland of wild flowers, which she had looped round her wrist. She walked a little way down the track, then clicked her tongue softly. There was a rustle in the undergrowth and out ambled the white horse. The woman hoisted up her sari and pulled the front up between her legs, as women do who work in the fields. Then she took the reins and led the horse to a mound which, when she stood on top of it, enabled her to mount. She took up the reins and called softly, '*Baita, aow!*' There was a scuffling overhead and the wild child swung among the branches and creepers, laughing and squealing. When she manoeuvred the horse beneath him, he let go and dropped neatly behind her on its back.

'Where are they going?' whispered Sparrow.

Bublu shrugged. 'Perhaps to find food?' He felt a little afraid. Strange that she should set off so late in the day.

It took two hours for the woman to reach the edge of cultivated fields, by which time the sun was well past its zenith. She stopped, just inside the shadows of the trees, watching. The wild child seemed content to doze behind her, his head resting on her back. She watched for a long time, her eyes seeming to consume every detail of the landscape and the humble low farming huts and sheds.

A line of women with pitchers on their heads trailed to and from the well; some with babies on their hips and children gambolling round them as they walked. Her body strained forward as if she thought she might identify some of them, but then she sank back, perhaps disappointed, but continued to watch for a long time. Finally, keeping within the line of trees so that she should remain unseen, the woman urged the horse onwards, moving round the outskirts of the village.

She knew her way well. She took secret paths, that only a local villager would know. She crossed through a part of the palace garden that had become wilderness, staying far from the sound of the rough voices of quarrelling boys and barely catching a glimpse of the palace walls.

The sun was lower in the sky and the shadows so long that they intertwined with each other. There was just a dull red glow of a grey rainy dusk when they reached the bungalow of the teacher. Here, the woman nudged the wild child. She spoke to him quietly then, taking his arm, lowered the wriggling boy to the ground. He stood for a while, as if reluctant, then bounded silently on to the verandah. She held up a hand in farewell, and dug her heels into the horse's flank and moved off.

Old Ram Singh shifted in agony on his bed mat behind the altar. He had taken to sleeping there, out of sight of the main door of the church. There had been an influx of Hindus and Sikhs into the neighbourhood, who had been chased over the border from Pakistan. It had brought confusion. In retaliation, local gangs hunted out any Muslims. Revenge still burned in the air. Often, his night's sleep was broken by the sounds of shouts and screams and the revving of alien trucks, which drove marauders into the village to do their worst, then drove them out again.

That night Ram Singh never quite let go of his consciousness. His senses were sharp and alert; his bones ached with a special intensity – they always did during the monsoon. He had gathered some bits of charcoal and twigs and lit his brazier, so that he could lie with his back to it, soaking up the warmth and easing his pain. He looked up through the flickering shadows to the white-washed ceiling, held up by black-painted wooden rafters. Through the darkness he listened to the rain pounding on the roof. Somewhere in the body of the church, he could hear the steady plop of water which had found an entry. Each drip fell ten metres and splattered on to the marble floor below with a resounding echo. By morning, he knew there would be more. He sighed, and thought of better days.

Suddenly he heard another sound, carrying faintly above the rain and the dripping. A woman's voice, singing; outside. He rolled over on to his knees and crouched, listening hard; persuading himself that he wasn't dreaming. He struggled to his feet, groaning softly and shaking his head with disbelief. What mad creature was out on a night like this? He took up the shawl on which he had been sleeping and rewrapped it round his bent body, then slipped his cracked, bare feet into his slippers. Painfully, he shuffled into the vestry and opened the small side door. The light of his brazier did not follow him, and he gazed out into a blackness that could, for all he knew, stretch for ever into oblivion. For a moment, all he could hear was the rain – that long, unbroken sound . . . on and on. Perhaps, after all, he had been dreaming or imagined it. But no. He heard it again. It was coming from the far end of the graveyard.

> 'Go to sleep, my baby.
> Close your pretty eyes.'

'Memsahib?' He had a sudden memory of Mrs Chadwick, kneeling each evening at the grave of her twins; telling them a story and singing them to sleep. But no, that was impossible. The Chadwicks had left long ago. He stood there, one hand soothing the small of his back. The voice went on singing. '*Mataji?*' He called a little louder. The song stopped abruptly. There was silence – except for the rain. After many minutes of waiting, Ram Singh hobbled back into the church, wonderingly. He went over to the old gramophone and selected a record, the one with the red label, and put it on the turntable. With slow, stiff fingers, he wound the handle and released the catch. The record began its seventy-eight revolutions per second and he placed the silver-headed arm, with its metal needle onto the grooves.

The sound of the violin was so loud, so piercingly sweet, the notes struck like arrows and, crouching on his old haunches, Ram Singh rocked with pleasure and sadness – and the pain of memory . . . oh, memory.

At dawn, he made his way down to the corner of the graveyard where the English twins, Ralph and Grace Chadwick, rested in peace. Lying on top of the grey stone slab, carefully arranged, was a fresh garland of flowers.

In the forest, when morning came, it was still raining. Bublu lay without moving, just listening to it as it swished like silk through the foliage. Then he heard the sound of undergrowth being parted. He remembered the woman. By the time he and Sparrow had gone to bed, she hadn't returned. Was that her now? He sat up smoothly, so as not to disturb Sparrow, who always slept moulded into Bublu's back for safety. The child was exhausted from looking for food yesterday, and they had hardly found enough berries and leaves to ease their hunger; so Sparrow didn't stir when Bublu got to his knees and crawled out of the hollow.

He saw the white horse. It was moving about through the wet trees, nibbling the leaves. There was no sign of the woman.

Bublu set about making his fire. He and Sparrow had stored as much wood as possible inside the dry hollows of trees. He piled up some sticks and leaves into a pyramid, then struck a match. A flame flickered greedily, and some leaves caught, spluttered and died. Everything was so damp. He cursed under his breath. He must guard his matches. Carefully, he struck another and held it to the driest twig he could find, until his fingers nearly burnt. The end of the twig smoked, it glowed, it burst into flame.

Now he pushed the burning twig into the leaves, and reluctantly, they began to smoulder too. Bublu crouched down and blew softly. Finally, little blue and green flames darted into the air and Bublu straightened up triumphantly.

He tended his fire for a long time, gently adding more and more wood to it as it gained in strength. As the pungent smell of wood smoke coiled up into the watery air, Bublu wondered whether the woman would smell it and be drawn out of her shelter, to see to her own fire. Usually, she was the first to be up. But she did not appear.

At last, Sparrow emerged, scrambling out in a panic, until he saw his protector, then he laughed with relief. He scampered round the fire like a puppy, and then something caught his eye, lying just near the entrance to their shelter. It seemed to be a parcel, wrapped in banana leaves.

'Hey, Bublu! Take a look at this!' cried Sparrow.

Wondering how he could have missed it, Bublu took the parcel and carefully opened it. Inside was a banana, a piece of dry chapatti and a dollop of dahl.

'Food!' breathed Sparrow faintly.

'It must be the woman. She must have brought it,' whispered Bublu.

'Shall we thank her?' asked Sparrow.

'Yes, of course, when she comes out. She isn't awake yet.'

They tried to eat slowly, to prolong the pleasure of having some solid food inside them, but it was gone all too quickly. They waited for the woman to come out, but she didn't, and the horse just continued meandering through the undergrowth, never really going out of earshot.

'Something must be wrong,' murmured Bublu. He decided on action now. He went boldly to the woman's tree and stood before the entrance to her dwelling in the hollow. '*Mataji?*' he called out politely. '*Mataji*, are you all right?' There was no reply.

'Is she there?' asked Sparrow. 'Perhaps she never came back.'

'The horse is there,' replied Bublu, 'and besides, who else would have left us this food?'

He crouched low and crawled, on hands and knees, inside the hollow. '*Mataji?*' he called more urgently. 'Are you there?'

As soon as he saw her, he knew she was ill. She lay on her matting with eyes wide open, glistening with fever. Her hair spread in a wet tangle round her face and neck, her arms outstretched as her body burned. He bent down at her side, but she didn't seem to see or hear him. He touched her hand – so hot was it, that he withdrew it in horror. '*Mataji?* What can I do for you?' Her eyes stared back sightlessly.

He backed out of the hollow and, picking up an empty cooking pot, ran down to the river with Sparrow chasing after him crying, 'What's wrong, Bublu? What's the matter?'

'The woman is ill. She has a fever. She burns. I don't know what to do, except cool her down. It's what my mother did to me, when I was ill.'

He pulled off his shirt and soaked it in the river

then, with Sparrow still at his heels, he dashed back to the hollow.

Suddenly, Bublu had a thought. 'Hey, Sparrow. You stay out here. I don't want you catching anything.'

'And you?' cried the child. 'What if you do? What would I do then?'

'Tch! Idiot! Stop being so fearful. Watch the fire for me. Whatever you do, don't let it go out.'

Hour after hour, Bublu soaked his shirt and dabbed the woman's head and arms, trying to draw the heat out of her body. He tipped back her head and tried to let water from the cooking pot trickle between her lips. Only when her eyes finally closed with sleep, did he creep away.

'Sparrow, I must leave you.'

'No, Bublu, no! You can't!' Sparrow shrieked with panic.

'Hey, you.' Bublu knelt down and took the boy firmly in his hands, holding him at arm's length and gazing steadily into his eyes. 'Do you ever want to grow up and be a man?'

'Yes, yes. Of course I do,' snivelled the child.

'Well, when do you think you start to be a man? How do you decide when it is right time?'

'When I'm older. When I'm as tall as you?' quavered Sparrow.

'No, Sparrow. It's not you who decides. Fate decides. Fate has decided today, now. You must start now, being a man – start by being a little braver, to set you on the right road. Do you see? I'm not abandoning you, but the woman is sick.

She could die. I must go to the village and get help. You must stay. You have two tasks; one, to keep the fire going; two, to keep the woman cool, and try to make her drink. Soak my shirt with water and squeeze the drops over her lips. I have to put you to that risk. Just don't drink from the same pot. I'll be back before nightfall, I swear.'

Bublu went into the undergrowth, clicking his tongue as he summoned the horse. There was a movement in the bushes, and the horse came ambling out. Bublu climbed on the mound and leapt astride the horse. He turned back once more. Sparrow stood there, frozen with terror. 'Hey, Sparrow! Promise me too, that whatever you do, you won't wander off. Stay near the fire – then the wild animals won't harm you. Promise? Don't let me down.'

Sparrow shook his head up and down vigorously.

Bublu dug his heels into the horse's side and set off at a canter, ducking beneath the low-hanging branches which swept over his bare back.

TWENTY-ONE

Promises to Keep

They called him wild, undisciplined, a savage; teachers had their own names for him, just as wounding as bandage-head, coolie or blackface. He wanted his revenge – and he got it, though not the way he had planned. He used to dream of burning down the school or praying that Mr Borden would be struck down by a terrible disease. But Jaspal's revenge came upon him far more sweetly. He passed the eleven-plus.

Mr Borden was disbelieving. Apopletic. Jaspal was a truant, a troublemaker. There had to be some mistake. He even telephoned the Education Authority to see if they had mixed up his papers. But there was no mistake. Jaspal had passed.

'Why, Jaspal, my boy! It looks as though you will be a scholar, just like your father!' Mr Chadwick said that with such pride and pleasure that Jaspal suddenly remembered the photograph of his father he had been brought up with. How reverently, over the years, he had gazed at the garlanded picture taken on the day Govind had received his degree.

Would he be the scholar and warrior his father had started out to be, but failed?

As if reading his mind, Harold Chadwick said gently, 'Your father was a brilliant pupil. He would have had such a bright future, if it hadn't been for the war. Forgive him, Jaspal. Don't punish yourself for what happened to all of you. You have a chance to be somebody – and make amends.'

But Jaspal's face was hard and blank, and Mr Chadwick could not tell what effect his words had had.

Govind was now living in a small bedsit in Richmond, not far from the the Chadwicks. He needed time to readjust to the outside world; time to realise that he could wake up when he wanted, eat when he wanted and have the freedom to go out and walk wherever he pleased.

Ever since Govind had left prison, he had begun to grow his hair. Already a moustache covered his upper lip and there was a deepening blur of beard growing round his chin and cheeks. Although his hair barely reached his shoulders, Govind now wore a turban. Among the few possessions which they returned to him when he left prison was an old cardboard shoebox. Inside were the comb, the sword and the steel bracelet. Govind Singh was retrieving his identity.

Every evening, he came to the Chadwicks to join them all for supper and they would discuss the future. Despite repeated letters to the authorities, and enquiries made by contacts living in the Deri district, there was no news of anyone resembling his wife Jhoti – either being listed as dead, or turning up in one of the camps. So now the plan was to go back to India in the autumn. This would give time for Govind to take a refresher course in teacher training, so that he could go and help Bahadhur Singh at the old school.

It was taken for granted that Marvinder would return too, but what should Jaspal do, now that he had passed the eleven-plus? They all talked animatedly of his future – and predicted that he could go to university and get a wonderful job.

'He should stay with us in England and go to the local grammar school,' suggested Dora Chadwick. She took her daughter's hand lovingly and said, 'We would like that, wouldn't we, Edith?'

'Oh yes!' cried Edith enthusiastically. 'I'll be so lonely if everyone goes away. Please stay, Jaspal – and Marvi too! Must she go?'

About Marvinder, Govind seemed adamant. 'Marvinder must return to India. Her future must be there. After all, what husband could there be for her here?'

Marvinder bowed her head.

Marvinder hadn't heard her mother's voice for a long time. Or perhaps, because she had been so taken up with thoughts of her concert and with thoughts of Patrick, she hadn't been listening.

'*I made promises. I promised I would wait. I would rather die than go back to our home without my husband and my children.*' Jhoti's voice penetrated her mind with such clarity that Marvinder looked up, wondering if anyone had heard.

Jaspal suddenly spoke in a low determined voice.

'I wish to go home. It's all I ever wanted. We must go back to our village. We will find out about our mother. Then I will learn to farm the land.' He got up and stood by his sister.

'*Praise be to God,*' *murmured Jhoti.*

There was a long silence, then Govind said quietly, 'That is what I want too. It pleases my heart to hear you say it.'

'*The monkeys built a bridge. It only took them five days – with the help of the spirits of the ocean, and then they were able to rush across, kill all the demons and rescue Sita. How long will it take you to cross the ocean, Marvinder, my child?*' *Her mother's voice sounded weak.*

'*Three weeks on the ocean, Ma, and then another few days before we reach our village.*'

'*Come soon,*' *said Jhoti, fading.*

'Is she very sick?' asked Bublu, as the teacher crouched in the hollow at the woman's side.

'Yes, very sick. If only she would let me take her to the village. My aunt would nurse her, and we could bring in a doctor. But she just will not agree to it, and I cannot force her.'

'I will stay with her here and nurse her till she is well,' Bublu said.

'So will I,' echoed Sparrow.

'I will come and visit you every three days with food. I will bring a charpoy, so that she may lie out in the clear fresh air instead of being inside that musty hollow,' said the teacher. 'But the horse will stay with you, and you must ride in and fetch me if you need me urgently. I will come by day or night.' Then he laughed and said, 'You two are like the princes, Rama and Lakshmana, guarding your princess Sita, hey? Just make sure that Ravana, the king of the demons, doesn't get her!'

'We shall make bows and arrows,' declared Sparrow solemnly. 'We shall kill any demons who come this way.'

A postman cycled down the long white road. He wasn't in a hurry and was rather glad of the two to three miles he had to cycle to deliver the letter. He enjoyed throwing his head back and singing at the top of his voice, while the wind flapped the cotton dhoti round his legs. Just before the railway track, the postman left the road and wobbled down the steep bank on to the path through the fields, which led to the village of Deri. He didn't often have to deliver letters to such remote villages, especially not letters from abroad, but today he bore a letter all the way from England. It had stamps with the King's head and it was addressed to Mr Bahadhur Singh.

The teacher received it with excitement. While his aunt gave the postman a cup of tea, he carefully slit open the envelope with a knife and, with nervous fingers, unfolded the stiff, white paper.

He stood a long while, motionless, reading and rereading the letter.

In front of the verandah, the wild child chased some chickens around the yard.. The postman sucked the hot tea noisily through his lips and stared at the teacher, burning with curiosity to know the contents of the letter. The aunt picked up her cane tray of lentils. She tossed and sifted and picked out the stones and tossed again, in a slow leisurely manner, waiting patiently to be informed of any news.

At last, the teacher came and sat down on the beach. 'Govind Singh is returning home with his children, Jaspal and Marvinder. Mr Chadwick is coming with them. He has permission to help me turn the palace into a school and I am to be its head and Govind, my assistant. He asks if I can prepare his old bungalow.'

'I have met thee where the night touches the
edge of the day; where the light startles the
darkness into dawn, and the waves carry the kiss
of the one shore to the other.'

A passenger in their carriage crouched in a corner. He was swathed in a shawl and his feet were tucked up beneath him, his chin resting on his knees. He recited the poetry of Tagore, his voice rising above the piston-hammering wheels of the train as it pounded across the vast plains of India. He observed the preoccupied silence of the father and the quiet, contained excitement of the children. Only the Englishman was prepared to catch his eye and nod his admiration of the poem.

'England is a land of poets too, eh?' grinned the

fellow-passenger. 'Shakespeare, Byron, Keats – isn't it?'

'Yes it is,' agreed Harold Chadwick, 'though I'm not sure how often you would find a fellow-passenger on an English train able to quote anything much.' He sighed.

The train hurtled on and on, mesmerising them all with its rhythms; sometimes breaking up into sharp multiple echoes as they passed a wood, or resounding through space as it crossed over a bridge. They were on the train for three days and two nights, journeying back into their homeland.

As they were carried into the state of Punjab, they all straightened with expectation. Jaspal stared intensely out of the window.

Between the folds of her veil Marvinder watched her father. Govind found it impossible to keep still. He walked up and down the corridor, sometimes leaning out of the window, as if he wanted to reach out and touch the landscape which stretched before him. At every stop, he got off the train and strode the platform from end to end, only jumping on again as the train began to move.

The violin case lay across her knees. It was the one thing she had been able to bring from England. Marvinder lifted the lid and touched the strings.

'Are you still there, Ma?'

Just before the third night, when all that was left of the sun was a blazing sickle slicing into the horizon, the train pulled up into the station of Deri. It was the festival of Diwali. The village women had taken special coloured powders and, sprinkling

247

it through their fingers, created beautiful, intricate patterns in the dust in front of their doorways and verandahs. They got dozens of little clay saucers of oil, in which they inserted a wick and they outlined their roofs and window ledges and verandahs and steps and paths, and when darkness came, they lit the wicks. All over India, there was a soft flickering, as they created a light powerful enough to over-come the demons; powerful enough to light the way home of those who had been in exile.

They saw the flickering from the train – a strangely white glow in the distance.

The teacher was waiting for them at the station with a bullock cart. They piled on their trunks and suitcases and then clambered in too. Jaspal sat up at the front with the teacher. It was in such a manner that they had left their village – it seemed like another lifetime ago – escaping in the darkness with mother and grandmother. Nazakhat had accompanied them a little way, but then finally, with an anguished farewell, had leapt in tears from the cart.

Jaspal gazed into the darkness all around him; remembering. Like Rama, they were coming home – but where was Sita?

'I want to find my mother,' whispered Jaspal.

The teacher murmured, 'There is a woman in the forest . . .'

The white horse was waiting in the yard. Within the soft light of the verandah lamp, it glowed in the darkness like jasmine. Bublu sat astride the horse and when he saw Jaspal, raised a hand in salute.

'Go with him, Nazakhat,' said the teacher, and lifted Jaspal up on to the horse.

Hanuman first disguised himself as a cat. He padded up the crystal stairways and across the marble floors, in and out of the silken chambers of Ravana's palace searching for Sita. When he couldn't find her there, he turned himself back into a small monkey, and leapt out over the balconies into the trees of the gardens beyond. All day long, he swung among the branches, dashed across green lawns and skirted the murmuring fountains, but he couldn't find her anywhere. At last, as daylight was fading, he came to the most distant and wild part of the garden, where thorns ripped at his fur and creepers trailed in confusion. There, where it was most desolate and abandoned, Hanuman found Sita. He leapt into the tree beneath which she was huddled and, coiling his long tail round an over-hanging branch, swung upside down so that his mouth came close to her ear. 'Sita, be brave. Rama is near. He is coming to rescue you.'

Jaspal knelt at his mother's side.

'Is it you, my son? My Hanuman?' she whispered.

'Yes, Ma! I have come to take you home. Father is waiting.'

OM
This is the Truth . . .
This is the sacrificial horse
Whose head is the dawn
Whose eye is the sun
Whose breath is the wind
And from whose open mouth
Blazes the cosmic fire.
In truth, this is the horse of sacrifice
Whose body is Time.

The Upanishads